AMERICAN TRINITY

& Other Stories from the Mormon Corridor

David Pace

Praise for David G. Pace

Pace's short fiction is affecting and illuminating. He writes unflinchingly, depicting those at the margins—the doubters, the diffident, and the disconsolate—with sensitivity, compassion, and humour.

- Carys Bray, author of *A Song for Issy Bradley*

There is deep pleasure to be found in the pages of David Pace's gorgeous collection of short fiction, *American Trinity*. These are moving narratives, steeped in wise and evocative contemplation, luminous with Mormon Americana. Pace deftly plumbs the sometimes dark, often difficult depths of faith and loss with an insider's knowledge and an angel's compassion. He is, without doubt, one of the finest storytellers to come out of the Mormon experience.

- Robert Hodgson Van Wagoner, author of *The Contortionists* and *Dancing Naked*

A former Mormon, David Pace with his deep concern for humanity and marvelous insights, brings members' struggles to light, showing how the LDS religion both feeds and strains the heart. These stories are brilliantly rendered, wildly funny and touching, as Pace reveals his characters' conflicts with their beliefs in Mormonism's rigid rules. We learn about the quirks of baptism of the dead, how sexual relationships are affected, as well as members' unique turmoils about leaving the religion, or going back to it, and much more. A lapsed Catholic, I feel that any Mormon or other person raised with strict faith, will love these stories as well as non-religious readers curious about the secret lives of the Mormon faithful, and unfaithful. I could not put this book down. Well-researched and intelligent, this is some of the finest fiction I have read about a religious culture, and some of the finest fiction I have ever read.

- Nancy Takacs, author of *Dearest Water*

David Pace's exhilarating new collection, *American Trinity*, fashions a new set of mythologies from the material of Mormon America—tales of doubters and believers, angels and heretics, the sacred and the profane. With wisdom and humor, these ambitious stories use the particularities of LDS culture and history as a lens to examine the most profound, universal elements of human life—producing a collection that speaks powerfully to Mormons and non-Mormons alike.

- Shawn Vestal, author of *Daredevils* and *Godforsaken Idaho*

This collection is dedicated to my wife, Cheryl Catherine Pace.

BY COMMON CONSENT PRESS *is a non-profit publisher dedicated to producing affordable, high-quality books that help define and shape the Latter-day Saint experience. BCC Press publishes books that address all aspects of Mormon life. Our mission includes finding manuscripts that will contribute to the lives of thoughtful Latter-day Saints, mentoring authors and nurturing projects to completion, and distributing important books to the Mormon audience at the lowest possible cost.*

American Trinity & Other Stories from the Mormon Corridor

For information contact
By Common Consent Press
4900 Penrose Dr.
Newburgh, IN 47630

Cover design: Jeremy Ames
Book design: Adam McLain
www.bccpress.org
ISBN-13: 978-1-961471-02-3
10 9 8 7 6 5 4 3 2 1

Contents

Foreword

CHRISTOPHER T. LEWIS

I love Three Nephites stories because, as befits the wandering trinity's reputation, they catch people off guard. Too often reduced to faith-promoting rumors or punchlines, the weight of their mythos can easily drag their exploits down into theatrics of parody or pageantry. Perhaps it is precisely because they are so easily reduced to a *deus ex machina*—coming to the rescue of the faithful with car trouble and giving warnings about food storage[1]—that midrashic or literary attempts to imbue them with "the full range of psychological and social complexity" have such promise.[2] After all, one does not expect to be confronted with much humanity in figures who, as immortal plot devices, encompass both God *and* the machine.

"American Trinity," the Three Nephites anchor story in this new collection by David G. Pace, resists the theatrics in favor of subtler theater in its approach to the foundational Mormon scripture, a juxtaposition that returns in the concluding entry of the book, "Caliban Revels Now Ended." From the disillusioned Nephite Zed, frequenting the theater district of Old New York, to a former missionary returning to his mission decades later to review a production of *The Tempest* (speaking of a *deus ex machina*), this book renders not just its Nephites but all its characters with a compassion that rises above the excesses of either *The Book of Mormon* musical or the Hill Cumorah Pageant. It is theater that, in the words of the protagonist of "Caliban," "transcend[s] both orthodoxy and disbelief."

Despite their cultural reputation, the Three Nephites are in fact an inspired point of departure for those in search of a nuanced look at the Restoration. Their role in Mormon mythology is less tied to orthodoxy than it first appears. True, on one level they function as the physical proof of The Book of Mormon's historicity that so many yearn for (see Rell in "Dreamcatcher"). As both participants in and witnesses of the text, they hold the potential to come forth at any time to manifest themselves as a powerful mark of its legitimacy. They tether an ancient account to the present because they exist beyond its pages. The idea that the reader could one day encounter one of them makes the story more current, more alive—more "for our day."

Even when the Three Nephites show up as angels dressed in white, the very fact that they represent a breach in the fabric of the world adds to its complexity. Neither mortal nor immortal, they are both liberated and confined by the in-between spaces they inhabit. They are time travelers who do not fully belong to the past or the present, caught between the mundane and the miraculous, history and folklore. They have existed for so long that they can no longer distinguish between the text of The Book and their own memories: "I remember little more about the Lord's sojourn with us than what anyone else can currently read, and I was there! That's what you call the power of a text," remarks Zed.

Zed himself draws attention to what most would consider

the standard faith-promoting narrative of Three Nephites folklore, which he refers to as "guerrilla ministering." He tags along with one of his brethren, Kumen, on a mission of comfort and aid to a lonely polygamous wife in the Ute Territory. When Kumen asks for food, she feeds him with the last of her cornmeal, which she had intended for her children. Kumen makes sure to hit all the right beats, replenishing her supply and disappearing before she has a chance to thank him. This is just the sort of event whose miraculous quality tends to escalate in the right hands. Zed, one of the scribes who shaped The Book of Mormon—and admittedly exaggerated that aspect of it—might have been tempted to add another layer to the miracle. If Kumen conveyed the woman's offering into the hands of her missionary husband on the other side of the ocean, for example, he would find himself in Maurine Whipple's Three Nephites story instead. "They Did Go Forth,"[3] archetypical of the genre in source material, approach, and augmentation of its scope, is based on an account of healing at the hands of a mysterious stranger from Whipple's own family history. She appended the transatlantic delivery of johnny cake for good measure.[4]

Neal Chandler's "The Last Nephite" at first appears to take a very different approach than either Pace or Whipple.[5] A comedic, modern-day encounter replete with corporate church trappings—hotels, business attire, security, files, corporate speak, and a general authority—the story even opens in the overflow of stake conference. A far cry from Zed's night at the theater in Old New York, with oysters, wine, and cigarettes, a cultural hall may be the most immediate setting imaginable: the spare and unglamorous heart of the institution.

Like "American Trinity," however, "The Last Nephite" leans into an association with those on the margins. Chandler's protagonist, who inadvertently gets caught up in the orbit of one of the Nephites, speculates that it is perhaps his little heterodoxies that provoked the visitation in the first place—not because the Nephite viewed him as a sinner, but because he needed an accomplice. In both these stories, the Nephites demonstrate that they are not bound by the authority of the Church. Rather, they regard it with some cynicism, and inhabit a space uncomfortably outside of the very hierarchy that draws its legitimacy from what they represent.

Authority aside, it is not just the company the Nephites keep who resist our assumptions about orthodoxy and orthopraxy. Zed is not above evil-speaking of the Lord's anointed—and not just any anointed, but Mormon himself. In Pace and Chandler, these special witnesses of The Book indulge in more than a little skepticism, alcohol, and polygamy. Simpson, the titular character in Levi Peterson's "The Third Nephite," is ugly, scrawny, foul-mouthed, wrathful, and most recently said to have been kicking around Las Vegas.[6] Todd Robert Petersen's Nathan Begay, a Three Nephites character in "Parables from the New World," surprises a Mormon sheriff by lamenting that The Book of Mormon doesn't contain tales like those about Old Man Coyote, who he suggests is gender non-conforming and into swinging.[7]

The tension between the inspiration, creation, and realization of a text is also a common thread in Three Nephites stories, diegetically and otherwise. Maurine Whipple enhanced hers for dramatic effect. Zed "made a point of infusing [The Book] with the requisite miracles." Simpson is accused of living in a story book, and, as we've just observed, Nathan Begay has unexpected opinions about the ideal contents of scripture. Tim Wirkus's *The Infinite Future* features three reclusive siblings caught between Brazil and Idaho, in a narrative compiled and translated from across many layers of nested accounts.[8] These siblings—the Coopers—hide behind a heteronymous author they have invented named Eduard Salgado-MacKenzie. As with the Nephites, Salgado-MacKenzie is more talked about than seen, and primarily known by the trail of works he leaves behind. Like Zed, the Coopers are witnesses to and participants in the production of a lost, but revenant manuscript—Mackenzie's novel, also entitled *The Infinite Future*. Though his book is not based on any real events (it's pulpy Brazilian sci-fi), that is in no way an impediment to it becoming a sacred text to others, and it proves as capable of inducing a mystical experience as The Book of Mormon. Ultimately, what the three Coopers create survives their collective authorship and the compilation and translation process to take on a life of its own, becoming more real than the story of its origins.

This is why Zed spends so much time dropping in on Mormon to harangue him. As in the Gospel of John, Zed is acutely aware of the creative, animating power of the Word. When he claims that what he "was fighting Mormon for was nothing less than my existence, my identity," it's not a figure of speech. Again referring to his own embellishments of The Book during his time as scribe, Zed knows how much the text will shape not only how he is remembered, but how he remembers, and not just who he is perceived to be, but who he is. Though he frets that "The prophecies of my people needed to be real instead of just a beautiful literary device," the danger or beauty of it is that they will end up being real no matter what.

Zed gives up the theater, but his inability to let go of his concern about the real leads him to seek out the Nephite god. Convinced that "the meaning of our lives has always been a construction," he wants to reorient himself with the sole remaining, stable reference point available to him. Still, even he acknowledges that what he wants is not the same as what he needs. Though the sleeping Nephite god drops into the text like a *deus ex machina*, He doesn't magically resolve anything. Zed finds him changed. Even He is not the constant Zed imagined Him to be. His wounds are healed. Their relationship has evolved: "I feel old enough to be the father of this sleeping god. That I have more to tell Him about His life than He can tell me about mine." Asleep as He is, He is unable to grant Zed the words of release he seeks.

But Zed reaffirms his faith in The Book. Up until this point he has chiefly been concerned with the authority of *writing* the text. But he finds his faith again in its power as a tool for *reading* one's life. The Book's performative nature doesn't flow in only one direction. Yes, when Zed does what The Book prophesies, he makes the prophecies true. When he remembers what was written in The Book, they become true memories. To some degree, he will always be subject to the Book's construction. But the Word that was God is not bound by time or perspective. It runs in both directions. Even I AM—the most powerful performative utterance of all—needs someone to read it.

So, as Zed and Kumen disagree about the difference between *remembering* what Jesus's directive was and what it *was*, Zed is onto something when he wonders about the possibility of redefining it later. If the life cycle of a text requires both author and reader, the reader's interpretation wields the Word with as much power as the author's. The constant isn't the text itself, but the wrestle with it, which can play out in myriad different ways. Zed tells the Nephite god that he loved him precisely because "you read my heart." And Zed recalls that the real danger of the Gadianton Robbers "was that there would be no record, no book to find oneself in." So, he weeps for his fate, but returns to his ministry. Of all the different worlds he is wedged between, the two most prominent are the written text and how it is read.

What makes "American Trinity" a fitting synecdoche for *American Trinity* is that, by foregrounding such a profoundly Mormon trope as the Three Nephites, it reveals the inherently marginal nature of those whom Jesus chooses. This is a powerful affirmation of individuals on the periphery of the institutional church, perhaps even of their Mormon-ness. When Nathan Begay articulates the predicament of the Three Nephites, he references this lack of belonging, but also goes on to suggest how it is valuable to their calling: "I got one foot in each world, Sheriff. It makes people nervous. Hell, it makes *me* nervous. Except everybody's caught between worlds, sheriff [sic]. Maybe it's the only thing any of us got in common."[9]

The fact that the Three Nephites can be drawn to people who, like themselves, are suspended between worlds is why they often succor those at death's door. For example, in Pace's novel *Dream House on Golan Drive*, Zed is called to watch over Riley Hartley, a Mormon who, at the end of his life has long since lost his faith and forsaken the Church. Zed's assignment is to "prevent Riley from approaching the veil prematurely."[10] Until Riley achieves some of the self-awareness that so torments Zed, until he can read himself and accept that he is more like his people than he thought, Zed cannot utter the words "Let him enter." (Notably, returning to church activity is not a condition.) That this should finally occur in a subway car under the East River further corroborates the Three Nephites' penchant for operating in the in-between. The Nephites' other companion, the wandering Jew Ahasverus, or Verus, echoes Nathan when he remarks to Zed that Riley is "a lot like us, if you think about it . . . because he's trapped, just like us."[11] But of course this doesn't only refer to the end of Riley's life—by then Zed had been shadowing him for a long, long time. As we've already seen, the thin edge between life and death isn't the only place to suffer on the periphery.

All the characters in the stories to follow have more than a few points in common with Riley Hartley, and the gay, cynical, carping, doubt-filled Zed is their patron saint. Since Zed is called to read the faith of the faithless, *American Trinity* may in fact best be understood as a collection of his wanderings and ministry. Zed's constant interrogation of himself, his calling, and what is real is essential to his mission among those caught between worlds. Outside of "American Trinity" and *Dream House on Golan Drive*, he may not materialize in the text, but we can read him into it.

Ultimately, Zed's wrestle with the reading of his own faith is his deepest expression of it, and the same can be said for everyone in this book. The details of each narrative are different, but, as Zed observes about the theater, the arc is familiar. Faith and unbelief, being in the world but not of it, being of the Church but not in it, orthodox and heterodox interpretations of a text—all Pace's wanderers are caught up in this kind of tension. It can be as simple as the consequences of the philosophies of men, mingled with scripture, as in "Mormon Moment." It can speak to the difficulties of living a divided existence, like the flight attendants (speaking of metaphors of not belonging) in "Robomaid" and "Flying Bishop." At a parting of the waters in one's life, it can take shape as the internal struggle between doing the hard thing and following the path of least resistance, as in "Sagarmatha." Or it can manifest itself in a supernatural, apocalyptic event, like in the magical realist fantasia "Angels in Utah," which sees names meant for proxy temple work resurrected to mortality and those intended to usher in immortality entombed instead.

"Lana Turner Has Collapsed!" also centers around the temple and the dynamic of inclusion and exclusion it inscribes on people's lives. Gloria has fallen into inactivity because, since she and her husband have no children, she has never felt like they fit into the "celestial picture." But when her husband returns to church and temple worship, she decides to give it a try as well, feeling a closeness to her mother as she prepares to do the temple work for the actress Lana Turner, in whom they shared an interest. But the experiment does not go according to plan, and Gloria discovers that she can't find a place among the living by way of the dead.

In "Stairway to Heaven," Jack Flanagan is neither alive nor dead. For as long as his body hasn't been found, a sort of limbo reigns. In this interregnum, the narrator muses about alternate possible versions of Jack that might've taken a different path. He hopes for a "ram in the thicket" for Jack and his family, but perhaps he is looking at it the wrong way around: Jack's death has sparked the narrator's first earnest prayer, which plants the seed of a faith more nuanced and compassionate than what he's experienced before. Perhaps the potential of alternate paths is for *him*. Alternate paths are also considered in "City of Saints," which portrays a man from one City of Saints (New Orleans) who has moved to another (Salt Lake City) after being called to the Seventy. Conflicted between his own instincts and the expectations of his position, and still sensing the lingering presence of his recently deceased wife, he demonstrates how not all evolutions of faith result in an obvious change of course.

"Dreamcatcher" intersects with many of the themes in "American Trinity," exploring the difficulties of handing down truth to the next generation, though by way of artistic and historical objects instead of the power of the text. Rell, a nightwatchman at a book depository, catches one of the dreams of his youth: coming face-to-face with the early Church and Book of Mormon relics that he had imagined would give him a perfect knowledge. But like most dreams, "It wasn't what he thought it would be." In a counterpoint between the Gilgal Sculpture Garden and a secret basement cache of all the Church's most sacred artifacts, Rell discovers that, as in "American Trinity," truth requires some active doing, and it's not necessarily safe to make the effort. (This story also involves a curiously specific parallel with Peterson's "The Third Nephite"—the juxtaposition of underwhelming relics with a bird falling down a chimney.)

In "Damascus Road," backsliding Mormon Paul invites a stranded Jewish stranger named Saul to share his hotel room for a night. This encounter with his doppelgänger from another world prompts him to reevaluate whether he ought to go back to church and confess his sins or be less afraid of venturing into unfamiliar territory. On the flight home, he catches the eye of a missionary giving away a Book of Mormon across the aisle and—perhaps because of his recent encounter with Saul—finds the exclusivity of the young man's message particularly grating. Turning away, he remembers a Russian poem he read in high school, which gives advice about what to do if one's parachute does not open:

> Spread your arms softly, like a bird,
> And enfolding space, fly.
>
> There is no way back, no time to go balmy,
> And only one solution the simplest:
> For the first time to compose yourself, and to fall
> With the universal void in your embrace.[12]

Certainly, there is no better description of what it feels like to be caught between spheres than plummeting to where the sky meets the earth, where one has no choice but to cross from one life to the next. And, for the most part, the characters in this book embrace their lot, as the poet suggests. Not without fear, not without suffering, but, seeing that there is no way back, they accept the unknown to come.

Caliban revels may not last forever, but Zed is right to wonder about the *when* of Jesus's promise that he and his companions will find "a fulness of joy." He wants an end so desperately that he is named for it. But like too many texts involving Jesus, this one, too, "is maddeningly unclear." So, all he can do in the meantime is give voice to the sorrow of his people—be they his lost immortal brethren, the descendants of Lehi, or the characters in this book. As Zed pours out his heart to the sleeping Nephite god, he takes credit for this passage in Jacob 7:26:

> "'The time passed away with us, and also our lives passed away like as it were unto us a dream, we being a lonesome and a solemn people, wanderers, cast out from Jerusalem, born in tribulation, in a wilderness, and hated of our brethren . . . wherefore, we did mourn out our days.'
>
> "I made sure that passage survived. That was my work. So that there would be a record of how it was like for this people. Of how we read this life."

Similar to Zed's own role in shaping The Book, some parts of this book began as non-fiction or have roots in real events. Others have been wholly invented. But they all convey the longing of those who are in some sense out of communion: lonesome, solemn, wandering, cast out, unrecognized by the Church or their own people. But they need not worry that there is no book that—transcending orthodoxy and disbelief—captures enough in-between-ness to find themselves in. David G. Pace has written it. That's what you call the power of a text.

---

1. William A. Wilson, "Freeways, Parking Lots, and Ice Cream Stands: The Three Nephites in Contemporary Society," *Dialogue: A Journal of Mormon Thought* 21, no. 3 (Fall 1988): 13–25.
2. Robert A. Rees, "The Midrashic Imagination and the Book of Mormon," *Dialogue: A Journal of Mormon Thought* 44, no. 3 (Fall 2011): 55.
3. Maurine Whipple, "They Did Go Forth," in *Bright Angels and Familiars: Contemporary Mormon Stories*, ed. Eugene England, (Salt Lake City: Signature Books, 1992), 11–19.
4. Veda Hale, Andrew Hall, and Lynne Larson, eds., *A Craving for Beauty: The Collected Writings of Maurine Whipple*, (Newburgh, IN: By Common Consent Press, 2020), 133.
5. Neal Chandler, "The Last Nephite," in *Benediction: A Book of Stories* (Salt Lake City: University of Utah Press, 1989), 166–94.
6. Levi S. Peterson, "The Third Nephite," in *Night Soil: New Stories* (Salt Lake City: Signature Books, 1990), 19–39.
7. Todd Robert Petersen, "Parables from the New World," in *Long After Dark: Stories and a Novella* (Provo, UT: Zarahemla Books, 2007), 49–58.
8. Tim Wirkus, *The Infinite Future* (New York: Penguin Press, 2018).
9. Petersen, 57.
10. David G. Pace, *Dream House on Golan Drive* (Salt Lake City: Signature Books, 2015), 51.
11. Ibid, 277.
12. Yevgeny Vinokurov, "When the Parachute Does Not Open," trans. Daniel Weissbort, *Poetry* CXXIV, no. 4 (July 1974): 190.

PART I
SALUTATIONS

American Trinity

The other two are more patient than I am. They bide their time. What's worse, Jonas is always telling me that I am shirking my duty. I haven't talked to him in over a century. Hundred and fifty years the last time I talked to Kumen. Even though I have returned to my mission of wandering and ministering, both would insist I've lost the spirit of the assignment. I avoid them now. I was just coming out of the Empire Theatre in Old New York when I last talked to Jonas. Word must have gotten out. Like myself, Jonas was dressed as a patron in tuxedo and gloves. Courtly old Jonas. "I like the collapsible opera hat," I told him. "Nice touch."

"You're playing with me, Zed. That I should even feel compelled to be here is an embarrassment." He looked about wild-eyed at the throng of velveted ladies and their escorts climbing into broughams parked under gas lamps.

"How long has it been?" I asked, putting on my own gloves. "The courts of Montezuma?"

"We go where we are called to go," he intoned. Then he looked at me, bemused. "You're the one holed up in the theater district. Shameful."

"Yes, but isn't it interesting that every time *you* decide to make an appearance it's where there happens to be a lot of social position? A lot of pretty ladies?" I said, nodding in the direction of another exiting entourage. "Even if it is an embarrassment." Jonas looked at me with practiced contempt. Then he asked me for one of the new manufactured cigarettes, for which I had recently given up my pipe. Convenience . . . plus I'd needed a change. Any kind of change. We walked down 40th Street, stepping over muddy wagon ruts.

In the restaurant, Jonas ordered wine and oysters while I smoked and studied the lace drapes on the windows behind him. Unlike Jonas who covets the world's beautiful artifacts, I am simply amazed that the living-who-will-die go to such efforts to create them at all. The crystal chandeliers brought over from old world Bohemia. The coffered ceilings of the rich. During the centuries of catastrophic Nephite wars, a man would intricately etch his sword as if his life depended not so much on the might of the metal, but on how beautifully it could kill. But as my two colleagues and I, left behind by edict, moved through the carnage with our amulets, our consecrated oils, our prayers, there was no way to see the wounded as dying beautifully.

Even when I was in Old New York with Jonas, the senior one, and eating oysters, I had surmised that this life we led was the way it was always going to be. For the Three Nephites, this was it. There would be no return of Jesus to mark the end of days and the end of our mission. That was why I was going to the theater—to escape. After three glasses of wine, I told Jonas that.

"You've lost your faith," he said.

"I've lost my life."

"Nonsense. The Lord has kept His promise to us. We are still here, aren't we?" He took another sip from the finely cut crystal glass and returned it carefully to the table. He leaned back in his chair and breathed in the night, then continued as if it were an afterthought.

"You've been here since the days of Zarahemla. A full life for us, if there's ever been one. We had families, children. Gave them our blessing before they went—"

"No," I interrupted, "*you* had children. *You* watched them die of old age. I had no children. I was always alone. I'm still alone." Jonas shook his head at me, the rims of his eyes pomegranate-red. I'll admit, when I received the calling nearly two thousand years ago, it seemed like a good idea—minister to the earth's inhabitants and then, at the second coming, go right into heaven, "in the twinkling of an eye," as The Book says.

"Perhaps you're lucky, Zed," he finally said. "It was merciless to watch my grandchildren die of old age. Even more so to see their grandchildren slaughtered needlessly."

"Maybe it *was* needed. Part of the history that must be written?"

"That's not what bothered me. There will always be wars. No, it was how they turned against themselves. And those bastard robbers," he spat, referring to the Gadianton robbers which still existed, a parallel order held together by secrecy and oaths and by the constant manufacture of an outside enemy to distract the people. In Old New York they were now called magnates. "Each of us is alone, Zed. You, me . . ."

"Not Kumen," I mused. "He has his fans." Jonas sensed my attitude. I had been watching too much Restoration Drama, and I was becoming a cynic.

"He likes it out there."

"He likes the desert," I said. "Unlike you."

"What do you mean?"

"He's probably eating locusts right now, on principle. Not exactly hot terrapin or oysters."

"We go where we are called to go," he repeated, annoyed.

"And also where there happen to be urban wonders and warm baths and . . . bottles of Bordeaux." I lifted my glass. He reluctantly toasted.

"I'm doing my time," he said.

"It *is* more like a sentence than a promise. And it's not over yet."

Jonas sighed, and pushed his plate away, the outline of his moving arm blurring ever so slightly in the air. It is the only feature that might distinguish us from others, a sort of full-body halo that lightly pulses around each of us and can only be seen by children and the occasional drunk whose vision is already failing at the edges. I am told that around my inexplicable red hair and fair skin the hue is pink.

"I really thought it was all about to end with the new age of prophecy," said Jonas.

"Never pin your hopes to a seer who secretly takes multiple wives. And in Illinois, no less."

"At least he translated The Book before he was gunned down. We have that, thank God. Maybe the end times are upon us after all?"

"Or maybe it's just a tease. A cosmic burlesque."

"You are a bitter man, Zed," said Jonas, and he drank the last of his wine. "Are you going down to the docks tonight?"

"I suspect there will be the sick to attend to. Where else would I be?"

"A box seat back at the Empire?" Now it was my colleague's turn to call my bluff.

❧

That was in Old New York, which doesn't exist any longer, and perhaps never really did—with all of its privileged, just another version of the Gadianton robbers, this time in spats. It was the last time I saw Jonas. Well, there was the Triangle Fire twenty years later, but I couldn't bring myself to speak to him then. I can always find him if I need to. But what do you say to someone you've known that long? Two thousand years as the American Trinity—it breeds contempt. But it's contempt with a residual ache for one another. So we routinely seek one another out, trapped as we are somewhere between deity and humankind. Mortal but unable to die. Angelic in our transport but plodding in our flesh. Embalmed alive. All of it set forth in The Book, the sacred history of the American continent.

Our story may not have a stirring ending—an ending at all—but it has a fabulous, inventive beginning. By the time I was born in Zarahemla, twenty-five years before Jesus made His New World appearance, my people had largely fallen out of favor with God; and in the turmoil, the Gadianton robbers could wreak their havoc.

In the midst of their intrigues, I was busy working in the temple scriptorium, a library of worn parchments. We were attempting to abridge them to something more permanent and had to compete with the armory for gold and other metals. I didn't think we needed another sword, another shield, however beautifully wrought. What we needed was the story. I actually paid attention to all the old tales I was transcribing. And I imagined what it was like to be one of my Hebrew ancestors, clambering into a ship and making the great journey from the Old World. I made a point of infusing the accounts with the requisite miracles.

There are worse things than doing that.

I was too slightly built to be a warrior. So I became the hands to my old mentor Omni whose fingers were permanently balled and ruined. He'd always seemed to care more about the written traditions than about war. And so did I. His work was to tell a story, to reset old writings into the plates of soft alloys and to interpret them for our day. Omni made us all part of a continuing tale.

"Show me a people who don't feel connected to their own biblical saga," he told me once, "and I will show you a people doomed to destruction."

But now, with the last of the precious metals needed for the war effort, the temple scriptorium was under siege. And Omni was failing. Lost in a fever, he lay against pillows in the corner of the room while I continued frantically to pound into metal the text from the papyri. So furious was my effort that my own fingers had begun to curl in on themselves. When the metal plates were complete, I bound them with rings and sent them out to be hidden from the enemy of the hour. You see, for the Gadianton robbers, it was always a classic "let's you and them fight." The Nephites were a nation hopelessly divided, and all the robbers had to do was give us enough rope and wait. That, and use our own schismatic warriors to do their dirty work. In fact, it was these warriors, lusting for gold, who were converging on the temple.

I heard voices outside. Before giving the last of the plates to the courier, I placed my hands on them and offered a prayer to the Nephite god for their protection. Suddenly, there were men everywhere in the room, their thick legs wrapped in leather and metal, their spears towering above me. On their heads they wore the traditional Nephite helmet, but their faces were striped with Lamanite paint. When they didn't find what they were looking for, they left, except for two of the men who took off their helmets and looked at me savagely. I knew it was my hair, an anomaly. Their mouths were wet and red with wine, their own hair long and tangled.

"You!" bellowed the biggest of the two, "hiding yourself here with a worthless old man who steals our gold while we fight his wars!" And with that he took his spear and slowly pressed it through Omni's chest so that his eyes opened wider and wider for one revelatory moment while he reached up with both arms as if to embrace a phantom deliverer. I could not go to Omni. Was it because I knew it wouldn't do any good? Or was I just afraid? Words, however, never failed me.

"Your wars have become the games of boys," I screamed, thinking I could shame them into silence. "You are Gadianton's lackeys, fighting for your own illusions and your own pleasure in death."

"Today you will die!" the warrior shouted.

"No, *you* will die—and all of this," I said, gesturing at the room of now scattered papyri and metal filings, "will be the only meaning left to your vandal lives."

That's the way the story goes. How it got recorded. Omni pinned against crimsoned pillows, my fear turned to outrage. I had silenced the thugs, but not because they were interested in "meaning," but in my person. They moved in on me, patting my head as if I were a house dog.

They took me by the hair, spread my legs, and raped me. After that, I knew I had to believe. Not only did the prophecies need to be saved for posterity, the story had to be real. Not just a beautiful literary device. They needed to be something that took place in real space, in real time where truth and accuracy aren't always contingent. The prophecies were that the Messiah was coming now, in a local appearance. That is how I remember it, through the record that now exists as The Book. That the Messiah would save me, Zedekiah, the red-headed scribe with the small hands.

Nothing like the grinding of another man's hips into your own to become a believer. It was clear what I needed saving from—an invading army, crashing through our homes and temples, and imbibing our blood.

And so it came to pass that the Messiah did come, out of the sky—a pinpoint of a man dressed in white and descending as if on a wire through a sky so dark that it was said you could feel it. In the ruins of the city, he stood, stretched out His arms, the wounds in His hands and in His feet still luminous and purple.

He was the most beautiful man I had ever seen. He came, and there was peace and prosperity (in the parlance of our time) even if it was for only a few years which would have suited me fine had I died within a man's life span. The span of life portrayed so well in the theater.

On stage it's like this. What counts is not so much what happens, but the arc of what happens between curtain rise and curtain fall. And, chiefly, there is the ending, a luxury reserved for those who will die. It's no mystery to me why, instead of tending to the needy or worse, slogging through the battlefields of collapsing nations as I am supposed to, that instead I sit clutching a playbill and watching the drama open, build to a climax and then end. The blessed ending. Maybe that's why, earlier, I cared so much about The Book. It had a life of its own. And it had to be recorded by someone—to be shaped. And so it was, by me.

I think there are worse things than fudging history. Like not having a history worth reading at all. I know the record kept changing because, for a while, I was the one doing it. He wasn't Jesus when he made his appearance. He was the Nephite god, and I'm okay with that. The story needing to be told was that we were Christ's "other sheep," destined to be brought into "one fold" with "one shepherd." I expected to continue as scribe, but then I was called to be one of His chosen disciples. Me, the small one with hair of fire. I was promised immortality as a kind of assist in the New World. Of course, I had to give up possession of the record, but I had had my time with it, and I refuse to complain about the scribes who came after me.

Okay, maybe I will. It's just that, as a scribe, *I* had a certain sensibility, a respect for the language, a sense of the record having continuity. Unlike Mormon. I can never forgive his imbecilic pruning of whole centuries of the story. "This army went here, this army went there . . . and it came to pass . . ." In his hands, a history became a kind of strident, outdoor pageant. He even cut the entire episode about Omni and the scriptorium. Granted, he was pressed for time during those final, desperate years of the Nephite nation. But did The Book have to be named after him?

"I have constraints of space and time," he kept telling me. And I would badger him, reappearing over and over in his tent, once five times within the hour.

"You're possessed," I told him once point blank. "You're possessed by military maneuvers."

"I'm a warrior," he would bark.

"A prophet-warrior. Like David, maybe?" I would suggest to him—to inspire him.

"He was no prophet."

"He was a poet."

"He was no prophet." Mormon was right about that. In fact David had forfeited any ready communion with his God. That's what made his songs so beautiful. The longing. The abject misery at being cut off. I like to believe that in the hereafter God will make an exception for a poet.

Maybe my hope for David is hope for myself. Maybe it was my hope for The Book that Mormon was hurriedly pounding out in condensed form from the voluminous old plates of Nephi—some of which I had translated myself in the scriptorium. The hope was that our mystical story of God's leading us from danger to a promised land might rival the Hebrew record brought out of Jerusalem by Father Lehi and the clan, even the Torah, or "Bible" which is today cherished above all other histories. Without our own inspired, and inspiring book, those of us residing in the New World would always be relegated to the step-sheep of God.

"We are more than just the sum of our battles," I would say, and storm out of Mormon's tent. Eventually, he got back at me. In his account of the three of us, left behind to walk the earth for century after dreary century, the old warrior-editor quipped that he had seen the three of us, and that we "ministered" unto him. I can't speak for the other two, but I did not "minister" unto Mormon. Harangued him was more like it. I was the one possessed by something. Mormon was about to die in battle, and I was worried about translation, emphasis, what certain people would eventually call *hermeneutics*.

Maybe we *are* the sum of our battles. But my battles are interminable, it seems, my immortality a curse. Before He rose to heaven, the Nephite god promised the three of us that we wouldn't die until He came again in glory to the whole world. He said, "And again, ye shall not have pain while ye shall dwell in the flesh, neither sorrow save it be for the sins of the world; and all this will I do because of the thing which ye have desired of me, for ye have desired that ye might bring the souls of men unto me, while the world shall stand. And for this cause ye shall have fulness of joy . . ."

Joy. But when? The text is maddeningly unclear.

I remember little more about the Lord's sojourn with us than what anyone else can currently read, and I was there! That's what you call the power of a text. So what I was fighting Mormon for was nothing less than my existence, my identity as a disciple of a god who battered our hearts into newness—

not just micromanaged ancient Meso-American battles. Mormon has gone on to his end and his reward. But all that I am, stretched out like a string over two thousand linear years, is in the permanent record that got left behind. I am the one, ministering around—longing like David—for some kind of ending to the story that *I* am still living.

It certainly doesn't feel like "fulness of joy." Jesus must have meant that joy would be our *eventual* reward. After we are "changed in the twinkling of an eye" at His second coming. I've had a mind to track Him down, to demand closure. But I am afraid it might demonstrate that I have lost my faith, as Jonas says. Maybe I am just terrified of what my Lord would tell me.

❧

None of this seems to bother Kumen. When he reads the one account of who he is—one of three Nephites left to wander and bring souls to the Jew Jesus who became Christ, the Son of God, and then God himself—he accepts the catechism without question, shedding all personal feeling, all memory. Like a coat.

For Kumen, it goes like this. A Jew or a Gentile—either one—gets into trouble. Kumen floats around until he finds one of these souls, believer or no, and he materializes. Brings a flask of water to save the dying-of-thirst, presses forgotten consecrated oil into the palm of the healer, enters the flight deck of the tumbling jetliner. He saves the day. Then, he dematerializes before they turn around to say thank you, vaporizes with their despair. This is the sign, the guardian angel thing.

I get the idea that this tickles old Kumen pink. Being sneaky, formulaic. I call it guerilla ministering.

"How do you know if that leads them to greater faith?" I asked him once in 1871, years before my dinner with Jonas. I had just seen a show called "Buffalo Bill" in New York and become curious how accurate the stage story was to the American West. So I just "happened" by one day in the Sierra Nevada when Kumen was about to blast through to a gold digger trapped in a mine.

"Of course it leads to greater faith. If you saw a miracle in front of you what would you think?" I lighted my pipe—still my prop at the time—and followed him into the mine, unseen. The man, in a fetal position lay near crumbled rock, his head darkly matted with blood.

"I might think it was Buddha, if I were Buddhist. Or if I were a superstitious Muslim, a jinni. That's not exactly working the program, if you know what I mean." Kumen took an amulet from his threadbare coat and placed it on the forehead of the man whose dusty eyes opened to the miracle above him. Kumen offered a prayer in the Adamic language that featured some impressive-sounding diphthongs, then he smiled gently at the man who sat up, the light from the lantern reflecting off the beatific face of my colleague.

Oh, the look in the miner's eyes! Even I got choked up.

"The problem with you, Zed, is that you are a humanist. You have no sense of what's absolute," said Kumen outside the mine where it was so bright that I instinctively manufactured a broad-brimmed hat to protect my notoriously pale face from the sun's rays. He slapped the dirt from his dungarees. Kumen had no idea what "humanist" meant. But he liked to use the term as a battering ram. "People just want to feel better in the moment. They don't want to actually solve their problems."

"Some of us want to solve our problems," I said, puffing on my pipe. I followed him east, holding my hat in the arid wind, to the pioneer settlements of the Ute Territory, where the people of The Book were congregating. Though he was third in the Trinity, he was the most diligent of the Three Nephites, based on the account of who we were supposed to be. As usual, I fell into the role of nag and hated myself for it.

We were standing outside a makeshift adobe hut. A polygamous woman came to the back door to shake out a rug. Kumen was there, asking for food. He knew, as she did, that there was only enough corn meal to make one small flapjack for her two hungry children. She took him in anyway and fed him. There was unanswerable pain in her sunburned, twenty-year-old face, a dissolute pain kept in check only by the ignorance of youth.

"Thank you, sister," Kumen said after his humble meal. He tipped his hat to her. When he left, the grain bin began to glow, and I knew what Kumen had done. A textbook miracle. She raced to the door to see who this strange figure was, but he was gone. Of course. We watched as she fell to her knees and wept.

"I'd say that woman—Sister Leavitt is her name—I'd say she has a life full of faith ahead of her," said Kumen, and he smiled. "That's what's real, Zed. Giving them something to believe in."

"What about follow-up?" I asked, folding my arms across my chest.

"Being able to tell her sister wives this little story about one of the Three Nephites appearing to her in her hour of desperation is all she'll need to carry on in this life. A scribe, in the year of our Lord himself, like you, should understand the power of telling a story."

"It's not that," I said. "I question your motives."

"There is no need for me to question my motives if I'm doing what I was called to do. We must be in the world but not of it."

"But you're doing all of this by rote. Maybe the reason people don't try to solve their problems—to really transform—is that they sense that for you there's nothing outside your silly standards. Not even their own experience, for heaven's sake." I could see that Kumen was losing patience with me, but I couldn't resist. "The interaction may be as much about you as it is them. Maybe they're supposed to change you as much as the other way around. Ever consider that?"

"The dogs bark, but the caravan moves on," he snarled, then reached over, ripped the pipe out of my mouth, and threw it to the ground. "Why would anyone take you seriously with that bowl of filthy weed in your mouth?"

"What do you remember Jesus's directive was to us?" I demanded, nonplussed.

"It's not what we *remember* His directive to be," Kumen said. "It's what the directive *was*. You're like one of those Unitarians, Zed, so embedded in the world that they're always distorting everything." He sighed. "You know as well as I do that it was to bring souls to the Christ."

"But what does that mean? Do you ever question what—"

"It means what it meant for *us*," he shouted. He clutched at his chest, breathing hard.

"But I don't remember what it meant to me," I said. "Not really. And maybe that's the way it's supposed to be. Maybe that creates an opportunity for us to redefine what it means. To tailor it to the circumstances, to the individual." Kumen sat down, still clutching his chest. He always did this when we debated doctrinal matters, apparently forgetting that we'd been promised we wouldn't suffer physical pain. I used to find it cute the way he would pant and moan, talk about his palpitations. But this time I was just annoyed. I looked around for my pipe.

"Do you know how much work you've avoided by fretting

over details non-stop?" he said finally. "You're a sophist, Zed. A Gadianton robber."

"Gadianton?" I spotted it, next to that rock.

"Exploiting the situation. Sabotaging the work. Sneaking around and sowing seeds of doubt, not change . . ."

"I'm entitled to a life, to my own experience, damn you. And don't forget that it was I who kept The Book from getting into their hands. That's what they wanted."

"And what have you done since then? I tremble to think of how disappointed in you the Lord is, Zed. The way you snivel all the time, it's enough to make me sick."

"Maybe the Lord is disappointed in *you*," I said, tapping the back of my pipe against my palm. "Your fly-by-night ministrations. Your—your sentimentalizing of Him into some kind of long-haired celebrity."

Kumen stood up, and I knew I had pushed him too far. He brought his right arm to the square to denounce me. "By the power of the Melchizedek priesthood I forbid you to demean our Lord and Savior."

Now that I was denounced, I had to leave. At least for the time being. That was the rule. So I did, muttering to myself and ashamed for mistreating one of my own brethren. Kumen always used that against me. Not the hand-to-square thing. No, he would question my character, my commitment.

Maybe Kumen is right. Maybe my sins are the greater, held captive by my own game. It wasn't the altruist in me that found the calling appealing or even the desire to share the taste of salvation. Maybe it was just that never dying would mean I could spend time pegging others—Kumen the fundamentalist, Jonas the executive—so that I would never have to peg myself as anything. What I didn't anticipate was that I would not only end up utterly alone, but that I was going to have to learn what it meant to die without ever actually dying.

And what better place to learn how to die than in the theater? *Medea*, *Hamlet*, Dryden's *All for Love*, the title of which says it all. That's when I took my little "holiday" as they say, which is why Jonas showed up outside the Empire Theatre to reprimand me. But I wasn't ready then to give up the theater and its artificial but seductive modes, and I didn't. Not until later. There was the stage at night, and the streets of New York during the day. I would look at the arriving immigrants, pathetic, frightened things, and wonder if I could extend the meaning wrought by the stage onto them and thus onto me. I thought maybe they held some kind of remedy to the agony of my loneliness in the promised land.

It was 1911, and I was still in New York. As I walked down busy 26th Street, I heard fire alarms, four of them in fifteen minutes. By the time I arrived at the Asch Building at the corner of Washington Place and Greene Street, several small bodies had already shattered the glass canopy covering the sidewalk, and were lying still against the hard pavement. All around, as the fire trucks arrived, horrified people were screaming "Don't jump!" at the girls huddled in ninth-floor windows pouring out smoke, a hundred feet up. But jump they did, some holding hands, their burning dresses blowing up over their faces, one dress catching on a wire where the girl dangled before the cloth burned through and she thudded to the ground.

Even I, who had ministered ankle deep in blood to the slaughtered Lamanites in Central America, who had cared for the Africans in the dark holds of slave ships, who held up the lolling heads of the bayoneted bodies in Lincoln's War—even I could hardly stand to watch children burning and falling while adults stood helplessly by. Then it occurred to me that all of the sidewalk crowd was an accomplice to this tragedy. An accomplice to an age that not only conveniently clothed and fed us but kindled this fire as well. And I, too, was an accomplice to this event just as the Nephites were to their own extinction.

I took off my jacket and hat and walked up to the largest pile of bodies lying in a pool of water from the fire hoses. The firemen had no time to attend to what looked like the dead, for a dozen more of the terrorized girls were still getting ready to jump through the smoke and haze and through the hopelessly futile fire nets, falling like overripe fruit dropping to the orchard floor.

I sensed that someone was alive in the pile. I wormed my way through the corpses, through arms and legs, bloodied and crushed, and near the bottom to where a twelve-year-old lay, her body twisted. Everywhere was the smell of smoke, of burned hair, of moistness all around. She lay quietly, her eyes open and afraid, her crushed chest still somehow rising and falling. I lay next to her and held her in my arms and tried to remember my prayers through fear that seemed to vault to the height from which my new charge had fallen. There was the little-girl smell in her skin, so different from that of boys, and I pressed my lips into the top of her dark, tangled hair.

"The finished shirtwaists caught fire," she whispered. "They were all above us, and they burned off the wires and fell on top of us, and the trimmings on the floor caught the fire, and the elevator was blocked and there were only windows."

"Were you afraid?" I asked. She could not look at me, because her neck was broken, but I could see the sudden sadness in one of her eyes.

"I was afraid when the others jumped. When I saw them

fall to the ground. It was not so bad when I finally did it. Am I going to die?" she asked finally.

"You are going to die," I said.

"Then I shall pray," she said, and it was then that I saw in her other hand a book in Hebrew she had obviously taken to the window and clutched during her plunge. She groped at the pages with one hand and her lips began to move. I held her tightly, making myself as small as possible under the pile of bodies—just large enough to do my duty, to see it through, while the final scene of her life closed in around her. I wanted to be witness, and maybe if I was lucky, to be a kind of comfort, to hold the only kind of child that would ever be mine—a dying one.

She stopped praying, and for a moment I thought she had passed on, but then I felt her hand reach up and touch my face. Without knowing it, and against all the rules, I was crying, and she had felt my shaking. She offered a prayer that I neither heard nor understood but simply felt through the points of her two small fingers pressed into my brow.

"Don't be afraid," she finally said.

When the men reached her, she was still breathing, but two minutes later, she expired. I watched as her spirit rose out of her, thinning to a shining thread, her outline momentarily blurring in the air. Blurring like ours does.

As they carried what remained of the girls away, Jonas was there, standing to the side of the crowd still milling across the street. As always, he was alone. I looked at him for a long time, ashamed, but somehow renewed at the same time. Had he come to discipline me, this senior member of the august Three Nephites? Discipline me for losing my composure while on duty? I turned away, looking up one last time at the now silent building, still intact. When I turned back around, Jonas was gone.

And so it came to pass, I gave up the theater after the drama of the 1911 Triangle Fire. In the theater, there is too much vicarious life on stage, thrilling in that pre-digested way—but instantly dismissible once you walk out the door. I hear that theatrical entertainments are quite the show now. With the invention of moving, lighted pictures on a screen, our relentless industrialization has turned technological. And dramatized illusions are so mesmerizing, they say, that daily life for some has become the intermission between cinematic moments. But illusions as such would have no power over me today, having simply made it obvious that the meaning of our lives has always been a construction. As in The Book.

That is why, today, I am no longer waiting for His return. I am going in search of the Nephite god, the savior of the world. I must see Him again.

It isn't as hard as I thought it would be. He is nearby, asleep on an antique, four-poster bed; and, lying there, He has that half-levitating look of someone dreaming, His body outlined under a sheet. I wait for him to wake; and for a moment, I feel again the ancient stirring in my heart from the days He lived with us. The adrenaline. The infatuation. Desires unaccounted for. But then I realize that, out of His setting, it just isn't the same. He is slighter of build than I remember, the shape of His face less angular, less strong. Freckles on His arms and chest. And the five special wounds on His hands, feet, and side are now scars, mere plugs to the punctures I once touched with my own hands. To touch Him, to touch His wounds, was to know that He understood me, what it had been like for me not just to be raped that day in the scriptorium, but all of it, to be the outsider with strange gifts and even stranger desires that never fit the way of the world—desires in the mind and in the body. To be childless. To be chosen as one of His New World disciples because He felt sorry for me.

"I want to die," I say to the sleeping form. "I want you to release me from my mission. I have seen too much. I've been here longer than you were." He stirs slightly, lifting His arm up over His head and twisting in the bed. I can hear His breathing, see His chest rising and falling slowly, the chest whose warmth I felt when He ordained and blessed me before he left us. But now, I feel old enough to be the father of this sleeping god. That I have more to tell Him about His life than He can tell me about mine.

"The threat from the Gadianton robbers was never disbelief, or even secret wars," I say. "No, the real threat was that there would be no record, no book to find oneself in. That was what they wanted to destroy. Not ourselves, but our literary selves. I may not be a believer like Jonas or Kumen, but I believe in The Book. I fought over how it got put down. Listen to the words: 'The time passed away with us, and also our lives passed away like as it were unto us a dream, we being a lonesome and a solemn people, wanderers, cast out from Jerusalem, born in tribulation, in a wilderness, and hated of our brethren . . . wherefore, we did mourn out our days.'"

"I made sure that passage survived. That was my work. So that there would be a record of how it was like for this people. Of how we read this life.

"That was why I loved you. When you were among us in the flesh, you read my heart. I thought you could see through this smallish, irritable man to one who loved the word, and the idea of you, and your grand entrances and exits. Who loved your continuity from beginning to end, from ministry in the Old World to ascension in the New. Who loved the way you died. Who loved your curtain calls. Who can't abide the way you sleep and dream now."

There are tears that suddenly water His image lying before me, washing the scene of any grand mystique. What I want is not the same as what I need. And so I cry for the lost Nephite that I am, and then lean and kiss my Lord good-bye, not as I want Him to be, but as He is.

The sleeping god smiles, and now I can go.

Stairway to Heaven

The day after high school graduation Jack Flanagan drowned in a water-skiing accident, and they couldn't find his body for ten days. They said that he may have still been drinking from the night before, which wouldn't have surprised me, of course.

When I was twelve, I hung out with Jack even though he was one of the kids whose family had money, unlike ours. As deacons we were required to show up periodically with the rest of the ward to work at a nearby welfare farm. One early Saturday morning we were supposed to be picking apples, an activity which I despised mostly because my father was at the time the ward welfare director, and his flannel-shirted zeal for energizing the troops embarrassed me. It was just like Jack—a tall, athletic boy—to "discover" half a package of firecrackers in his coat pocket, but that I was the one he confided in with his contraband somehow gave me a sense of importance from this rich, Snob Hill kid that I couldn't resist. With Jack by my side, his thrilling wickedness as natural as a laugh, I became an instant hoodlum.

We edged our way down a few rows of trees, out of sight of

the other workers, and Jack showed me how to imbed a firecracker in a decaying apple, light the fuse, and then throw it up over the tops of the trees where it exploded, saucing the ward members below. Shortly afterwards, Brother Leavitt came tearing through the trees. He found us, on the ground three rows away from the rest of the pickers and nonchalantly dropping apples into our empty buckets.

"Which one of you did it?" he thundered.

"Did what?" I asked, pulling on my most innocent face. I didn't blink an eye. Brother Leavitt just looked at us both, his forehead and hair bearing the effects of the exploded apple.

"You'll pay for this someday," he said, looking right at Jack who was having a hard time stifling a laugh. I elbowed him discreetly. I was obviously better at this part than he was.

"Pay for what?" I asked, and I put an apple to my mouth and bit down on it. Not once did I take my eyes off Brother Leavitt who eventually turned and walked away, his hand searching his back pocket for a handkerchief.

After the apple escapade, I was invited to Jack's thirteenth birthday party, a frenzied, Nerf football-throwing affair at which I presented him with an Andy Capp book of comics (his favorite). Soon afterwards, however, it was as though the shallow prospector's pan of early adolescence began to aerate our fears, and we became more and more suspicious of each other. Or maybe it was the gospel that got between us. I had a testimony. Jack Flanagan did not. For one thing, rich or not, Jack liked to swear.

Once, at school, he told me he'd been walking down our street at two in the morning and saw someone in front of our house dancing under the streetlight. At first, he told me, he thought he was hallucinating, but when he got closer he realized it was my sister Jocelyn, who at seventeen never wore anything but full-length, homemade dresses and, like Mom, had taken to ballet.

"She was barefoot," he told me. "I go up to her and ask if she's okay. It's two o'clock in the fuckin' morning. Know what she said?" I shook my head, terrified of what he might tell me. "She says, 'Transcend. Purify. Glorious.' and then she went, like, twirling away." Jack clunked through a tippy-toed pirouette in his tennis shoes, his arms above his head, then laughed, reddening at his burst of animation, mimicking my sister in front of me. It occurred to me later that Jack, all bombast, was lonely, that he was seeking something he thought I had, and was embarrassed by the need. I had a secret envy of Jack and his facility for what my younger sisters would have called his "bathroom words"—and worse. Even so, this is what I said to him, quoting the current prophet: "Profanity is the effort of a feeble brain to express itself forcibly." Jack just looked at me, then walked away alone, as I did, but in the opposite direction.

I never told Jack that the dreamy response from Jocelyn, who had a reputation for being stridently expressive, was a direct lift from Neil Diamond's musical interpretation of *Jonathan Livingston Seagull*.

The next time I heard about Jack was after we had all turned sixteen and that he'd taken a corner too fast coming up the hill in his Datsun 280Z. He ended up in the kitchen of the Jorgensens. When Brother Jorgensen, clad only in his temple garments, came clattering into the kitchen half asleep to see what the heck was going on, there was Jack and his girlfriend, working on her cuticles, and still sitting in the car next to the Frigidaire. "Not my best moment," Jack had said to no one in particular. Janie Jorgensen said that the kitchen clock was still plastered on the front bumper the next morning like a hood ornament, its hands still pointing to that fateful moment, 2:23 a.m.

When I was on my mission, I sometimes thought of Jack, how he might have gone on a mission had he lived, that he might've repented of his sins like the rest of us had and gone to Mexico or Japan to serve the Lord. (He was certainly of a zealous type. At least when it came to his sports car.)

❧

Day five, still no Jack, no body floating near the north shore, or near any shore, and Heather Hintze, who was sort of in love with him, was driving by the house. She stopped to tell me that her old seminary teacher in an effort to comfort her had told her that Jack's mission was not on this earth, but in the spirit world where missionary work must continue for the salvation of the dead. Heather was standing behind the open door of her Camaro, the engine still humming, and I was in my bare feet on the street. I wondered if that could be true, if Jack could have been whisked through the Veil for a higher purpose.

When I told Dad about it, he dismissed the whole thing. For a short while he and I had been home teachers to the Flanagans, who by Dad's standards were only marginally active in the church.

"That is completely inconsistent with the Gospel," Dad said with his typical earnestness. He did not like Brother and Sister Flanagan, especially when they would end our visits with them impatiently rather than waiting for Dad to wind down. "Jack was headed down the wrong road. And dying doesn't change that."

I thought Dad might say something like that. I think that's why I told him. But something jogged loose in me as I drove off Snob Hill not sure where I was going. I ended up at Provo harbor. It was dusk. There were rescue vehicles, men drinking coffee, standing there in uniform and huge boots. I wondered if Jack's family was there, camping out, waiting each night for something other than tired recovery guys coming back for the night with their limp flashlights and shaking their heads. Was Jack's little sister here as well?

But I didn't see Brother and Sister Flanagan, and there was yellow tape at a certain point, so I turned around and headed back towards home. This wasn't some kind of competition, I realized. Either with Jack or with my Dad. Or with some congregation of rich church members driving to sacrament meeting in their BMWs.

That was the first time I can remember praying. Really making an offering at Father Abraham's vacant altar. I prayed that Jack's mother and father . . . his little sister . . . might figure out something in spite of what I thought (that Jack had been taken for a godly reason), and what Dad had said (that he wasn't worthy to have entered spirit paradise). And if there was something I could sacrifice to find Jack alive or at least redeem him in the hereafter, it would be the ram in the thicket, once I figured out what that ram might be. Nothing that would be too humiliating for me, of course, but, you know, some*thing*.

They say Jack's body was completely black by the time it surfaced without the aid of dragging hooks. No ram found. Or was there? He did have one heck of a send off. I guess money can buy you that. For three days afterwards I fantasized about my own obsequies, determined to have *Stairway to Heaven* played for the weeping crowd, just like Jack did. His little sister, a girl also named Heather—a freshman, I think, in high school—rode in the back of a black Lincoln Continental on the way up to the cemetery. I walked by on the way to my own car, a Ford Falcon that had a hole in the floor through which slush from the winter road sometimes sloshed.

Robomaid

Perhaps you wouldn't mind so much getting the parking tickets but you are already having such a bad day. By ten that morning scheduling has denied your trip drop so that you can't help your best friend move to Phoenix this weekend. Plus your sniffles from the day before have congealed into a full-blown head cold. Flight attendant and blocked ears—not a good combination. You feel cheated getting a cold so early in the fall. January maybe, but late October?

You've got problems.

And now the tickets, not one, but two are on the windshield of your silver-gray GTI which needs new struts, one other bad thing quickly piling up with others into something truly exasperating. The night before you parked at a curb on First Avenue zoned from 8 a.m. to 6 p.m. as two hour parking only. And when you arrived shortly after twelve—as in four minutes after twelve noon—two tickets were stuffed abruptly behind your left windshield wiper. It is a terrible sight for your mid-afternoon eyes which for a split second you think surely must be seeing double.

But male flight attendants, categorically in the minority at the airline, are not allowed to feel sorry for themselves. You are a Dick Cavett-type of guy, sensitive, understated, someone whose first thought after looking over an unfortunate scene is to blame yourself. Anyone will tell you that. Your contrition is a coded affair, Sunday after Sunday at the ward house. It's only in your hotel room on a layover far from home that you rake up your walkman and air guitar to Black Sabbath and Judas Priest.

Catharsis for a frustrated "sky gypsy" trapped in a Mormon body and destined to sling hash down the aisle of a Lockheed-1011 Tri-Star on the way to Honolulu ("Chicken or beef?" "Feather or leather?") and no harm done.

Earlier this year you blamed yourself, aloud to anyone who would listen, for not being able to save the life of a heart attack victim on a flight to Boise. "If I just hadn't hesitated," you'd brooded. "If I'd just pushed harder on the compressions," you'd speculated. The beefy guy, the one with the crew cut and the seen-it-all air about him, he'd told you point blank when you got back to Salt Lake that he and the other paramedics wouldn't have done a damn thing differently. But you'd owned the failure from the moment Cherry, her lipstick smeared across her left cheek from rescue breathing, told you the guy was turning from blue to gray, *that* kind of gray.

No air guitar that night.

You pick up the tickets off the windshield, and scan the carbon-copied scratches on the citation. You look at your watch. More despair. The second ticket has been dispatched just four minutes ago. A sense of injustice seizes you. There it is, that closed-in telescopic bitterness you rarely indulge in now beckoning you. Perhaps it is the mounting pressure of your studied self-control, your "emotion management" now beginning to crack. Yes. Your determination not to let the crush of irritable airline passengers get to you at work.

Last week, while working a full flight from Tampa to LaGuardia, you took the furious insults of a New Yorker with what appeared to be steady calm, with not so much as a flaring nostril. The passenger was steamed that he didn't get the aisle seat he requested three weeks earlier when he made his reservation. So his rage mushroomed. You could actually feel the heat emanating off his narrow, flushed face as he lasered a steady stream of expletives at you in the middle of the Boeing 757 aisle. After that sally into flight attendant hell, you calmly walked to the first class cabin, smiled at the lead flight attendant who was amazed at your handling "an unfortunate situation so well," entered the lav, and puked. At the layover hotel AC/DC is your choice. Before bed, "Shoot to Thrill" repeated. For forty-five minutes:

All you women who want a man of the street
But don't know which way you wanna turn
Just keep a-comin', and put your hand out to me
'Cause I'm the one who's gonna make you burn
I'm gonna take you down
Oh, down, down, down
So, don't you fool around
I'm gonna pull it, pull it, pull the trigger . . .

The room mirror smokes. You're smokin'. Next morning, back into the uniform. Calm as a summer's morning.

You look up from the tickets held in your hand and, in a move that will, in retrospect, seem too affected for your carefully crafted serenity, you snap your head to the left, looking East down First Avenue.

Meter Maid! Just one block east she is twinkling in her

postman-styled vehicle, clicking along, a thick stick with chalk on the end, marking with wide, yellow streaks the tires of cars parked along the curb. She stops momentarily, then moves ahead, the little box-of-a-truck with the left-sided steering wheel leaping forward from the high idle, brooming along to her next four-wheeled irritant.

Suddenly, you are jamming the keys into your car door, muttering angrily to yourself. "If she thinks she's gonna get away with this outrageous. . ." Through the windshield of your car, Meter Maid's rotating light refracts, and for a moment the scene rears up to you, surreal and distant. Ire suddenly vaults in you.

Dick Cavett gone screaming bonkers.

You speed away from the curb, the struts of the GTI still creaking badly. (And this, *after* you've dropped four hundred dollars down on State Street to have them fixed.) You are heading toward Meter Maid who is turning up the hill on "E" street, moving surprisingly fast. You accelerate. Since you have moved downtown you have been vaguely aware of the strict enforcement of parking violations in revenue-thin Salt Lake City. While browsing books at the Cosmic Aeroplane on First South you have periodically heard the cashier cry, "Meter Maid! Meter Maid! Meter Maid!" And you have seen patrons drop books, magazines, tapes and posters and charge out to the street, their arms flailing, to drop a quarter in the meter. But, you have noticed, if Meter Maid has started to write the ticket by the time the patron arrives at the side of the car, he or she is twenty bucks poorer, and nothing that is said to Meter Maid will cause her to relent. Nothing!

You see Meter Maid turn left on Fifth Ave. You follow frantically. She turns around half way up the street in a three-point maneuver, scooting over to the other side, stopping abruptly at an older Monte Carlo sitting languidly on the narrow street at the curb of a run-down blue townhouse. You pass her, spying a parking space directly behind the Monte Carlo. You turn your car around, with some difficulty, your struts screaming in pain, and park along the curb. But barely have you climbed out, barely have you raised the two tickets upward for emphasis than Meter Maid shoots away, bouncing and crunching gaily . . . cruelly. "She needs new struts too," you say as the distance between the two of you increases.

You leap back into your car, whacking your arm on the steering wheel. "Fuck!" you wail with such a successful sense of piercing injustice that you say it again, louder, just for good Ozzy Osbourne measure. "FUCK!" Meter Maid is out of sight or—Wait!—is that her bumper, rounding the corner on "F" Street? "I hate Meter Maid," you say with a brief return to some sense of calm. You are still breathing hard, but, by all appearances, at least momentarily, you have regained your composure. "I *hate* Meter Maid!" you say louder.

The term "Meter Maid," you will muse on later is a term singular in nature but which means all maids of the meter, who, attempting to fill their quota each day, tag and mark the unassuming automobiles of the city with vicious insensitivity. It is a term like "the Media" or "the Court" or "Legion." "We are Legion," said the devils to Jesus before he cast them into a bunch of carousing swine. "We *are* Meter Maid."

Up ahead is Meter Maid. This time she is standing next to a yellow Dasher which you can by now distinctly see cowering below her. Probably just slightly older than you, Meter Maid wears what appears to you to be leather, black and form-fitting. Her hair, shiny and blue-black sits immovable upon her head like a helmet. Wrap-around glasses with lenses black and terrible melt into her face above a jaw line as angular as the monotonous street grid of the City of Saints.

Now is your chance to extend the words and sentiments of

humanity, of the common man, typically brow-beaten by the Corporate State, to demand a hearing, to exact justice—all of this presented to The Beast, to the executor of a crazed system, to a revenge-sick Meter Maid.

You park, exit the GTI and approach her. Think Dick. Think Dick Cavett.

"Excuse me, are you C. Post?" you manage to say, referring to the compressed signature on both of your tickets. Meter Maid nods coolly. Name must be "Carmen," you think, Carmen Post, a name with ominous overtones. "I understand that I was parked for more than two hours. But why the second ticket, if you don't mind my asking?" You pause. "I mean, I *live* on First Avenue." Meter Maid looks at you, at the tickets which you are holding just slightly aloft—for emphasis—then at the GTI behind you, her head moving slowly and exercising a kind of eerie command on the scene.

"Excuse me?" she replies with a delayed, stoical mien. Just the kind of thing someone named Carmen would say. After all, wasn't it in the opera "Carmen" that the title character stabs her lover to death?

Well, somebody gets stabbed.

In the lenses of Meter Maid's sunglasses you see a shrinking reflection of yourself, truncated, puny. Around your feet swirl leaves, orange and red, in rivulets of rust. The air is chilled. An early winter is coming on, and it is only the last week of October. She climbs back into her truck.

"Why do I have two tickets?" you add, advancing a couple steps. Meter Maid shifts her weight in the truck and seems to sigh. "Because you were there for over six hours." And then, with some sarcasm and a lift of one of her dark eyebrows she says, "The first two were free."

"You mean to tell me that every two hours I'd get another one?" You tighten your jaw just a little so that she won't see it trembling with exasperation. Meter Maid nods. The thought of forty dollars perforates your mind, then pulses like a yellow traffic light. Easily, a tank of gas, that's what you're out.

"If you'd come out before I'd gotten to you I would've waived the second one," she hisses. Meter Maid shifts from neutral to drive. Then suddenly she's gone in a creak, a bounce, a swoosh with the autumn wind.

Ashen, you stand in the middle of the street. A burning sensation creeps into your gut the tighter you clench the citations in your left hand. They feel moist, oily from perspiration. Your head is congested from your cold, and you suddenly have to pee badly. Maybe kill her with kindness. (Are you losing your focus?) Maybe offer her sexual favors. The thought of pressing your body against the cold, steely frame of Meter Maid glances off the corner of your mind.

Though only half resigned to the idea of paying your fines, you get back into your car and drive down the hill. You drive slowly, your brand new Pirelli tires rolling, limping, in defeat beneath you. You turn into an Albertsons, a large, blue-signed place with a trashed parking lot. "I hate this place," you mutter as you park next to a loaf of white bread thoroughly mashed into the greasy blacktop. And then you scream, "I HATE THIS PLACE!" A woman in a soiled, Kelly green parka is pushing a cart filled with groceries, her fussing child pulling at a plastic bag. She looks at you with surprise, then contempt.

But you will hardly even notice the mother and child. In fact, you will notice precious little except that in your rear view mirror is the passing image of . . . Meter Maid!

You don't remember starting the car back up. You don't remember shifting into reverse, then first. You don't hear the squeal of your tires or the screams of the woman whom you narrowly miss as you charge out of the parking lot and onto

Fourth East. You only remember thinking life would be a very hard thing to live from now on.

At the intersection of Sixth South the light turns yellow. Meter Maid doesn't slow. Before she gets to the intersection, the light snaps to a red. You roar up to the light and slam to a stop. You're breathing hard, and you feel the blood surge through your jugular and into your tightly wound head at a frenzied rate. You see visions in front of you, of your Boeing 757, silver gray, bearing down on Meter Maid's now distant, absurdly twinkling truck, escorting her to a forced landing at your pleasure. No. Destiny is now wielding an ax: you will hurl your jet at five hundred and fifty miles an hour—cruising speed—through her back window and, simultaneously, in one move of your hand, you will reach out and grab Meter Maid's throat before both ticketer and ticket-ee roll together out in the salt flats of the west desert in a screaming fireball.

The light changes. You grind from one gear to the next, faster and faster until you're suddenly screeching to a halt just short of Meter Maid's bumper.

"What the hell are you doing?" screams the startled Meter Maid. She leaps out of her truck. You will not leap from your GTI. You will emerge like a squinting Clint Eastwood, fingering his gun. She is wearing boots, black leather ones, but the rest of her leather outfit is suddenly gone. Meter Maid is now without her glasses, and her blue eyes flash angrily so that you think, with a sudden interior lurch, that she is strangely beautiful. Her hair is soft with an auburn tint to it in the mid-afternoon sunshine. "You could've killed me!" she screams.

Now you are standing there, suddenly spent and a little dizzy, as if all around you the world has fallen completely silent, as if you were on a stage and have forgotten your lines in a high school play called "Out of the Frying Pan." A kind of emptiness fills your stomach, and you feel that you're going to retch, just keel over the hood of your GTI that you're standing limply next to and cough blood. "You . . . you ran a red light." Breathing . . . labored. "I could issue you a citizen's arrest. I could haul your ass in and . . . and you'd be history. Ha! And you, a public employee, breaking the law!"

Meter Maid is younger than she was earlier, with woundingly full lips. She looks like somebody's daughter who has a degree in interior design and kisses her Dad good night when she's home visiting. "Give it a rest, buddy," she says, looking at the crumpled tickets in your hand and shaking her head incredulously. "You're going to get in trouble, here. Leave me alone or I'll call the police!" The shelf of her bosom heaves underneath her shirt. You blink into the shock of sunlight. Is she the same woman you'd initially approached? You can't tell for sure.

For a moment you wonder where you are. Is this Boise, or Phoenix? Think Dick. Think Dick Cavett. You turn to get back into the car, feeling that familiar contraction of control return but with it a sense of loss. You can't take the loss. Fuck Dick. Fuck Dick Cavett.

Turning back around, you square your shoulders with Meter Maid, clear your throat and channel, appropriately enough, Motörhead.

It's not until you are into the third line of a song titled "Sweet Revenge" that you see her respond at all, and then it is just the tiniest twitch in her left eye.

You press on.

Hello victim!
I can almost taste it

It's the need to see you die

You thought you had it made
Well here's your final shock surprise

You grab your crotch. Obscenely. There's no turning back now.

How do you like it

My unfaithful friend?

By now you've figured out that you are about to finish in a different key and at the requisite metal rock bellow which rings from off the nearby building and turns the heads of half a dozen people in the street.

How do you like it?

How do you like my sweet revenge?

sweet revenge.

By the time the final syllable fades, protracted in the late morning air, the silenced Meter Maid has returned to her seat, her back to you. You hear the click of her seatbelt. You return coolly to your cockpit, slam the door, slip gently into first and throttle down the runway.

Damascus Road

"I am a religious man," Paul told him for the second time, through the haze of too many Bass ales. "I can help you." The man, in his *kippah* and orthodox garb, squinted up at him, mouth twisted, fringe from his *tallit* dripping off his sides like old pasta. It was Friday night in midtown Manhattan.

The Jewish man started in again, not really pacing up and down 7th Avenue, but turning this way and that, gesturing downtown from where Paul had come, weaving from the Irish pub near the Sheraton in his drunken grievance. Now Paul had a situation. Not just a street person asking for money, or the time of day. Here was an inconsolable man, playing off his innocence to the big city just as Paul was.

Am I religious? thought Paul. *Still?*

No one would be answering the phone at the yeshiva upstate. Having been relieved of his wallet by "filthy homeless people," the man explained to Paul, he hadn't had the money to take the bus back before sundown. He had said this with much woe, wagging his head which, though bearded, was missing the extravagant, curled *payot* typical of many of the orthodox in New York. The man was visiting from Tel Aviv and wanted to see the city. Now this.

"I went to the police. I sit there for two hours, then left," he said through an accent, his hands drawn to his face, covering his eyes as if trying to transport himself away from the city by not looking at it. The January wind was picking up. He drew his dark wool jacket around him tighter.

Paul turned toward his own hotel on Lexington, walking the man back with him.

The visitor, finally quieted, sat in the upholstered chair and smoked a thin, stinking cigarette. Paul sat on the bed in the tiny room, the beer in his head finally clearing. On the way back to his room, Paul had to find a place to pee on the cross street to the hotel—between a parked town car and a backhoe at rest. Returning, Paul had put his arm around the stooped, frightened man who was close to his own age, to reassure him. He had told him that he had done a kind of pilgrimage to Israel when he was in college and that more than once he had been to Tel Aviv on business. That being a religious man himself, he understood the difficulties one's faith could present.

What Paul didn't say was that, like his impromptu guest, who would be spending the night with him, he too was violating the rules of his creed. First there was the drinking and whatever he was going to find in the direction away from the Irish Pub that night—a sex shop, a prostitute?—and then there was the fact that he hadn't been to church since his divorce three years earlier.

"What line of work are you in?" Paul asked, to get the man's mind off his troubles. The man squinted at Paul. "What do you do in Tel Aviv?" Paul rejoined. "You know . . . *job*?"

The man stubbed his cigarette out in the makeshift ashtray. "Lawn furniture," he said. "My name is Saul. You are a kind man." He worried over the cigarette butt, rubbed it into the bottom of the glass until the flecks were scattered like ground pepper. "I can repay you," he continued. "When you are next in Israel, you will be my guest."

They readied for bed. Saul sighed and stood to unbutton his shirt, draping it over the back of the chair. He turned his back to Paul. Looked around. Then he removed the fringed *tallit katan* which he folded carefully and set aside. Paul pretended to arrange something atop the bureau. In the mirror he could see Saul's back, a profound uncertainty welting his shoulders. Finally, Saul stripped off his sleeveless T-shirt. His chest and arms were stout, with coarse, black hair. Paul turned, removed his own overcoat, then his sweater and shirt, revealing the scooped neck of his cotton undergarment and its tiny, stitched symbols—the compass, and the square—one over each breast. The two men looked at each other.

"I can shower?" Saul asked.

"Of course," said Paul. (What else could he say?) "Towels are there." He gestured toward the bathroom. Saul turned to drop his pants to the floor. Underneath he was wearing skivvies, a sort of bikini bottom in the wildest colors Paul had ever seen—fuchsia bands and hot pink swirls over dark purple. Still, Saul's *kippah* rested on his head as he disappeared into the bathroom. "Will you switch light on for me?" he asked, returning momentarily to the room and suddenly looking elfin.

Paul flipped the switch for Saul and pulled the door shut behind him. He looked at the bed. A full, not even queen-sized. Were they really going to sleep there tonight? Two men? Complete strangers? What was he thinking of? He looked through his luggage. Zipped it closed. Then opened it and placed his wallet inside. Zipped it back closed. He turned around, and Saul was standing there in a towel. His *kippah* still atop his head. He pulled his skivvies back on under his towel, dropped the towel and got into bed. Only when he was lying on his back did he carefully remove the *kippah* and place it on the bed stand. The light burned above the headboard.

Paul flipped the bathroom light off. Saul lay in bed, the sheet pulled up under his chin, hair on his knuckles. Paul removed his pants and stood there in his thin white temple garment, extending to his knees. Symbols not only on each side of his chest but over his belly and right knee. Saul looked at him curiously.

"Christian?" he asked.

"Sort of," replied Paul. They stared at each other, until Paul felt the tired, ancient need to explain himself. "It's like a second skin, sort of," he said. "I think I might," he gestured at the chair, "stay up for a bit?"

"I'm sorry," Saul said. "I can sleep there."

"No," said Paul. "I want it this way. You need your rest." After a moment of looking at each other, Saul turned away in the bed. Paul picked up one of the pillows then reached up over the bed, and turned off the light.

"Thank you," he heard Saul say in the dark.

Settling into the chair, Paul pulled his overcoat up over him, settling in. The booze in his blood had long left him. In place of it was the dreary promise of morning. Within thirty minutes, he woke up with a start on the floor, in a fetal position. He went to the bathroom. Looked at the bathtub, then returned to the chair. Finally, he crawled into the bed next to Saul, listing to the edge. There was the squeaking of the springs, what seemed a cacophony of shifting starched sheets which kept him from the awkward silence he knew would ensue once he lay still. He was just so tired.

Saul talked in his sleep. In Hebrew, or was it Yiddish? Paul didn't know. At one point Paul found Saul's hand between his legs. He placed Saul's hand back where it belonged, and rolled to his left. Later, Paul rolled into Saul, spooning him, the hair on Saul's legs pricking him. Saul shook him off, so that Paul got up. He took off his garment top. Then fifteen minutes later got back up and put it back on. The garment was something he could not bring himself to permanently shed, despite his backsliding, but still wore hidden under his clothes even when he was out drinking and whoring. Lying there, wide awake, he thought about all of his secrets. And then, before finally drifting off to deep sleep, he thought of the morning and the erection he would inevitably have. He figured that Saul, observant Jew or not, would suffer the same break-of-day affliction. It occurred to Paul that they were both circumcised.

The next morning, Saul seemed less agitated, but still eager to return to the yeshiva despite it being Shabbos. The ox was in the mire, right? Didn't Saul believe in some version of that? Or, for Paul, was that just a euphemistic rationale back home for breaking the Sabbath whenever one wanted? No matter. Saul had to get back upstate. Now.

It was early. The two men had gotten less than five hours of sleep, if you could call it sleep. They dressed. Paul offered to walk Saul to Port Authority for his bus. On the way, Paul thought to buy Saul a coffee. Saul fidgeted just inside the door of the coffee shop, as if his very presence in a place of commerce on the day of rest would bring down the wrath of his God. Paul handed him the covered cup and started for the door, but Saul bee-lined for the sugar and cream. Ten sugar packs total. Paul counted them.

At the bus, Paul talked with the driver briefly, then gave Saul his ticket and a twenty. "The driver will tell you when to get off. Can you walk from there to the yeshiva?"

Saul nodded, then took out a pen and wrote his name and phone number onto a scrap of paper he picked up off the platform. "When in Israel?" said Saul. Standing there, Paul knew he was just the goy with whom Saul regrettably had to spend the night, but he took the paper anyway and nodded.

On the way back to the hotel to get ready for his cab ride to the airport, Paul walked slowly, his head aloft like a balloon above him from the night before. It was the Sabbath, but not *his* Sabbath. And he determined that when he got back to Salt Lake—away from New York which always seemed to bode trouble for him, to confuse him—that he would go back to the ward house and confess his sins to the bishop, or . . . maybe he would just relieve himself of his temple garments once and for all, cut out and burn the symbols as required before throwing the sacred underwear away. His second skin.

Hours later, he awoke on the plane. He could hear the drone of the engines outside, and the air vent above him. But he could see nothing, as if he were suddenly blind. He heard a voice. He remembered the eye shades, took them off, and was blinded again, but this time by daylight. Outside the window the earth was flat, etched with giant, fallow circles of farmland. Out near the horizon, rays of light shattered into haze. His head still throbbed.

Suspended as Paul was, he wondered what he would do with himself when he got home. He looked down, but the prairie below had no answer for him. He thought of Saul back at the yeshiva. Did he have to explain to anyone what happened? How or why he had broken the Sabbath? Did anyone actually care?

He heard the voice again and understood. "Yes, and I

testify that Joseph Smith did see God the Father and His son Jesus Christ."

"In upstate New York?" asked a second voice.

"That is correct. In Palmyra New York, and what's more I know that you too can know as I do, without a shadow of doubt, that the church the Prophet Joseph established is the true church."

This was what had awakened Paul to the emptiness outside his window and in his head. Across the aisle sat a woman, holding a blue paperback book he recognized all too well and next to her a young man in a white shirt and tie, scrubbed ears all aglow, a look of divine frenzy in his face. He caught the missionary's eye, or did the "Elder" catch his? Was this a sign? thought Paul. And then he felt a keen resentment about it all. Whatever "all" was. *Fastest growing church in the world!*

He repositioned his eye shade—lights out—and turned his head away from the scene. He thought of how close he was, all of them in this flying tin can to instant death just beyond the thin skin of the plane. It reminded him of a poem his high school teacher had scratched into the blackboard back in the day. A poem he thought of often, actually about tugging at the ripcord and the parachute refusing to open. What does one do? Paul would panic at first, of course, thrashing and screaming, but then he would stop, per the poet's suggestion. Breathe in the view, open his arms wide, tranquil as the sky above him and the earth below and for one single moment the universal void would be within his embrace.

PART II
ACCOMMODATIONS

Lana Turner Has Collapsed!

. . . suddenly I see a headline
LANA TURNER HAS COLLAPSED!
[. . .]
I have been to lots of parties
and acted perfectly disgraceful
but I never actually collapsed
oh Lana Turner we love you get up
- Frank O'Hara (1964)

"How was the temple?" asked Gloria. Her husband Don had just spent the late afternoon dressed in white and saving the dead.

"The way I remember it, for the most part," he said. "More computerized." She looked at him blankly. "The recommend, you know." He reached for his wallet and pulled out a thin white paper folded in half and housed in clear plastic, about the size of a credit card. Gloria leaned in, studying the paper with the church's cumbersomely long name stacked on top of itself, the name of her husband, the ecclesiastical signatures scrawled at the bottom. Don smelled of sweat and cologne—that new generation of cologne she'd gotten him for his birthday, hoping to add a little spice to their life after twenty-one years together.

"I don't get it," she said, moving toward the refrigerator and pulling an apron off its hook in a single gesture—the apron with the silk-screened torso bulging under a watermelon-patterned string bikini. A joke for her birthday. "A little larceny," Don had said to her the day she unwrapped it, nose scrunched. "A little larceny for our little life," he'd said. And she'd collapsed it into her lap with a smirk, shaking her head.

"Little life" was code for their life of routine. A truncated life of casseroles and green beans, Friday night dinners at The Old Spaghetti Factory, and childlessness.

She walked back to Don, pulling the apron over her head, tying it behind her back. She snatched the recommend out of his hand. "What's this strip on the back?" she asked.

"When you enter the temple, they slide it through a reader," he said, leaning in. "It records that you're there." She dropped it on the table in front of him. He picked the card back up and studied it as if he might find something hidden he had missed earlier. "My name is magnetically encrypted on this strip, and when you run it through, you know, it links to a database." She politely waited for him to finish but was already formulating her response.

"And if you're not part of the system, two very nice men from the mafia turn you right around and show you the door?" She turned back to the stove, stirring hard macaroni into boiling water. She looked at him over her shoulder and grinned.

"Now why would you say such a thing?" he asked. He was prepared for this.

"Say what?"

"Gloria," he said, in his new vernacular of pleading. (They *were* talking about religion.) "You should come with me. Let's go together. Today I went through a session for a man named Joseph Forsythe, born in 1832. Maybe he was a relative of mine. Or someone famous. Who knows?"

She trained her sights on her husband just as she did on artwork and prints at work, on the endless family portraits with grandchildren popping out of them like seedlings. What she saw was a man in his late 40s, his white shirt crumpled, his tie askew. He was thickening, yes, but still topped with that Yorkish moor of black hair; still the man with whom she slept. Then she looked at him like she had thought of looking at Michael at the frame shop, fifteen years her junior, whose swimmer's body he could barely contain under his T-shirt. She imagined she was someone—not herself—who better fit into the cartoon bikini she wore on her apron and who wasn't shy of guiding a swimmer's body into the dark back room where they kept the mouldings. Framing with purpose. Was it the vision of Michael, his broad back and worn jeans that now made her husband look like a boy himself behind his glasses, even with his five o'clock shadow?

How she wished she could have given her husband a child. Given herself a child. She didn't want to save the dead like Don was trying to do, a bizarre practice that Mormons, replete with passwords and secret handshakes, had been doing since the mid-1800s. She wanted to save the living. To save themselves.

That night, Don dreamt he was walking down the street. It was the 1930s and all the men wore hats pulled down so that he could barely see their faces. The streets were muted gray like those Great Depression-era paintings he and Gloria had seen the week before at the museum—hobos in boxcars, a dejected man sitting on the curb, gray flannel legs moving briskly past behind him. In Don's dream the tide of men in hats flooded the street, and Don strained to look into each face. Perhaps, he thought, I'm looking for Joseph Forsythe. Attach the name to a face. The face of a man who is in search of something that will rescue him. Then one of the men looked up and stopped in front of him. He was smoking a cigarette. His face opened into a crooked grin, a pencil mustache crackling above his lips. The rugged look, the dark hair. The eyes. It was not Joseph Forsythe. It was Clark Gable.

The next day, Gloria was eyeing a photo print the size of an oversized desk blotter, the woman across from her old enough to be her mother. "Sister Baker," to use the respectful term with a fellow Latter-day Saint.

"We don't want anything to take away from the portrait," Sister Baker said. She tilted her head at the print that was, to her, upside-down on the counter. "The photographer insists that it be very simple, maybe a black metal frame?" Gloria knew she was being asked to provide a different opinion. The woman didn't want anything like a black metal frame, and probably not anything "simple." Gloria scanned the composition, a grouping of over a dozen people, Sister Baker and her smiling husband at the center, one hand of each clasped tightly and resting in the woman's lap. The family was impossibly good-looking. All dark hair and gleaming white teeth. Like the Osmonds.

"Well," said Gloria. "As a designer, I would try putting on more than one mat." She turned to collect corners in various shades of gray: an off-white one; something warmer. Returning, she noticed that the woman was looking at the displays of framed pictures on the far wall. Gloria placed three mats on the upper right-hand corner of the print, each with a one-eighth-inch reveal, then turned it so that it was right-side up for her client.

"What about something like this?" Gloria heard from across the room. Sister Baker was pointing at what Gloria referred to privately as the Manic Titanic, five mats of varied reveals and a five-inch wide, bright-white shellacked frame, dwarfing the picture of a smiling, Nordic-haired family. The frame alone would set someone back six hundred dollars.

"I like this one," said the woman. "It speaks to . . ."

Your ostentatiousness? thought Gloria, pursing her lips.

"It's very glamorous," Gloria said out loud after a beat. The woman was trying to read Gloria, who was very good not only at design, but at telling a story to her clients that would make them walk out of the shop believing that not only did they get a deal but that they had an artistic gene that would rival Michelangelo's. ("That's why everybody's framing around here looks like the flippin' Vatican's," she had often complained to Don.)

While she took the woman's contact information and wrote up the work order, Gloria closed the deal. "You have such a lovely family, Sister Baker. All of them are simply gorgeous. Like their parents." She looked up over her glasses and smiled. The woman smiled back politely, still trying to figure her host out.

"You don't think this will overwhelm the picture?" the woman asked, peering at the gargantuan assemblage. Gloria looked thoughtfully at the arrangement—the sample corners, the mats—all under the full spectrum light she had positioned over the project.

"Well, it might be a little bright, Chloe," she said, this time opting for the woman's first name—more intimate. She came around to the other side of the counter and gestured across the expanse of smiles and the dark, brooding garden behind them. Gloria could tell by her expression in the portrait that Sister Baker was not really "there." One of the grandchildren, perhaps fifteen, and one of the sons—Don's age?—carried a certain gravity behind the smile that spoke of something profoundly unfinished, even disturbed. "The frame complements the composition, I think. The white frame, the gloss. It makes everyone's teeth really pop." The woman adjusted her glasses, leaning into the portrait then leaning back. Gloria waited, looking into her client's face. Sister Baker smiled and nodded.

"You're right," she said. "Thank you!"

"No . . ." said Gloria, continuing in the script. "Thank *YOU*!"

Gloria sat drinking her coffee and thumbing through a magazine. She was early, taking a long lunch break so that she could talk to Trudy who was just finishing up with her eleven o'clock. Sister Bodell sat in the chrome and padded hooded hair-dryer. She looked like a prune with a giant bonnet on her head, the traditional style and set that, it being 1995, seemed more than outdated to Gloria. Grotesque, she thought. Just like her own name: antique and grotesque. Like something out of the *Dick van Dyke Show*. In spite of this, the old woman was smiling away, quite pleased to be under the caring, skilled hands of her trusted beautician, who kept checking on her, smiling conspiratorially. Who am I to judge Sister Bodell? Gloria thought. This could be the highlight of her week.

Trudy extracted Sister Bodell from the hair dryer and helped her back into the swivel chair where she dropped like a sack of sand. She turned her client around to face the mirror, and after working a brush expertly through her hair, sprayed the woman's bouf, now dyed a gentle blue. "A regular Lana Turner," said Trudy finally, her hands resting lightly on the woman's shoulders. The two of them smiled into the mirror. It was the very picture—even a framed picture, thought Gloria—of sisterly affection and the commerce of beauty.

While Trudy took a phone call, Gloria walked Sister Bodell to the door. "Trudy has made you look like a movie star," she said as she helped the old woman on with her coat. She asked how her children were doing, her grandchildren. They now numbered thirty-two, she learned.

"Oh, my. You are lovely to help me. Bless you!" Sister Bodell said.

"And it's pretty darn sexy, if you ask me," Gloria continued. She couldn't resist spiking her language a little. Sister Bodell leaned hard against Gloria as she lowered herself down the steps to the walk, but then she didn't let go. Suddenly, her tone changed, as if someone had flipped a switch. "You know, Gloria, the only regret I have since my husband died is that I didn't suck on his penis the way he always wanted me to." Gloria coughed. "I loved that man," continued Sister Bodell. "But when I asked the bishop whether it was allowed, he gave me one of those priesthood lectures. Said that I should not be behaving in bed like a pole dancer." She gripped Gloria's arm harder. "What does dancing have to do with it? The dope was almost young enough to be my grandson. Imagine that. And telling me that I couldn't suck on my own husband's penis?" She let go finally, hiked her purse up over her shoulder, and moved toward her car. Then she turned, and in a stage whisper said, "Give him what he wants, sister. Don't wait until you're living with regret like me." Gloria watched the LTD lurch away from the curb.

"You're the only one in here who drinks coffee," said Trudy when Gloria returned to the shop—and her mug. "It makes everyone uncomfortable, you know."

"And it's lousy coffee," Gloria quipped.

"Like I say. You're the only one. And if the bishop finds out, he'll be calling you in." Trudy shook Sister Bodell's hair clippings from the plastic covering and readjusted a large aluminum hair pin on the rolled-up cuff of her sleeve.

"Only among the Mormons could drinking coffee turn into a social statement," said Gloria, collapsing into the chair next to the sink. "I need something more up-to-date, Trudy," Gloria sighed, her back to the sink. She looked at herself in the mirror opposite, turning her head from side to side. "Don's gone back to the temple, and he wants me to go with him."

Trudy tipped Gloria's head back. "Mid-life thing going on? Couldn't he just buy a fast car?" Gloria closed her eyes and took a deep breath. The water gurgled and sprayed. Negative ions elevated her mood. Twenty, thirty years from now she would be Sister Bodell getting her wash and blow-dry once a week and walking out of the Wildflower Salon smiling beneath her helmet hair. That was as good as it was going to get for her.

Trudy sat Gloria back up and wrapped a towel around her shoulders, dabbing at the strands. "Let's get you ready for your close-up," she said. Gloria smiled at the reference to her namesake, Gloria Swanson, in *Sunset Boulevard*. The age of glamour and Hollywood royalty. A simpler time, it seemed to her. Black-and-white photos of women in shirtwaists gazing back at the world in a way women had never gazed before. Poised. Arch. Confident. A construction, but still appealing. Gloria was hungry for that. Five years ago, she had asked herself, since there would be no children, why did she and Don still "dress the part"? The lumpen, thrown-together couple with four, five, six, even seven kids in the back seats of a Suburban? She and Don were a traditional-looking couple that wasn't traditional. A husband and wife who could not fulfill the covenant they'd made when married in the temple to "multiply and replenish the earth."

"Trudy," said Gloria, again facing the mirror, "why are Don and I trying so hard to look like everyone else when there's no room for a childless couple in the celestial picture?"

"At least you have someone to go to the House of the Lord with," Trudy said. Her fingers threaded through Gloria's hair; it looked strangely ragged now—wild. "My sister Stella told me the other day that she went to the temple for someone named Amelia Earhart. Now . . . what are the chances that she did that sacred work there for *the* Amelia Earhart?"

Gloria thought for a second. "Pretty good, I would say. How many Amelia Earharts do you know of?"

"Exactly."

"You can do that?

"Do what?"

"Go through the temple for a famous person?"

"As long as they're dead. Everyone needs saving, you know."

Gloria thought about this for a while.

"I've heard that Marilyn Monroe has had her work done at least ten times," Trudy continued.

"No!"

"You heard right, sister. Ten different people have gone through the temple believing that they were the Blonde Bombshell."

"The *proxy* for the Blonde Bombshell," Gloria corrected.

"Yeah. Whatever."

That night, Gloria stood in front of the bathroom mirror waiting for Don to come home. The meatloaf sizzled in the oven; the side of frozen peas steamed atop the stove; the half-gallon of Snelgrove's sat in the freezer; and she wasn't happy with her hair. Trudy had cut it short, with long bangs reminiscent of the 60s that swept over from left to right over one of her eyes, and she was feeling self-conscious. She combed it, fluffed at it, held herself in contempt, turned her head to see how it looked from this angle and that. She sighed, put the comb down, picked up the brush, looked at her reflection again, sniffed, slammed the brush into a drawer, and slammed the drawer shut.

She turned. There was Don. "Nice hair," he said tentatively. "*You* like it?" She pushed past him, toward the kitchen, embarrassed now for real, still touching at her hair. "Dinner's about ready. We just need to make the salad."

At the kitchen sink, Don moved behind her and looked at them both, his head floating above hers in the window's reflection. His hair was tousled from the day, sideburns nearly to the lobe of his ear, pursuant to the current style. And Gloria? She looked like Lulu from *To Sir with Love*; right out of London's East End but without the miniskirt. It turned him on; but no one would have known. Being aroused, even by his wife, was a mere synaptic blink that tingled in his scalp then dropped south where it dissipated in a twenty-year sea of responsibility and resignation. It had been a long time since the tingle had settled in his testicles, a problematic region for a man like him anyway—especially one who had just returned to the temple without his wife.

Still, there was this vision of them as a couple in the window—and the hope could spread, couldn't it?—through his chest and end-of-day shoulders that Gloria had gripped in days past when she rode on top of him during sex—a position that seemed especially thrilling at the time.

In the earlier days. Especially when they were still trying to get pregnant. Yes. That. Glorious Gloria, the love of his . . .

"I've gone back to doing our genealogy," she said suddenly, tearing at the lettuce in the sink. "Did you know that you're related to some famous people?"

Don was rising back out of his balls and into his head. "Like who?"

"Like Clint Eastwood."

"Dirty Harry?"

"Through his mother's side. Third cousins, once removed."

"Never could figure out what that meant," he said. "Once removed instead of just second cousins. And please don't explain it to me again. I can never remember the difference."

Years earlier Gloria had taken a nosedive into the family group sheets, the pioneer journals, the old Books of Remembrance. It was shortly after they'd returned from the doctor who had told her that there was something wrong with her eggs—or their behavior, anyway. The way they failed to make it down the correct tube and attach to the correct layer. The next weekend she had headed to Gunnison and raided her Aunt LaRue's den of old papers, sepia-toned photos, birth certificates—all painfully pasted together into a kind of crude family album. Gloria had sifted through the den and returned with five boxes of stuff, becoming the *de facto* family genealogist. Soon she was called by the bishop to be the family history specialist in the ward before she abruptly asked to be released a year later and stopped going to church altogether. "Genealogy is too time-consuming," she had told Don. "Everyone who's into it is a fuddy-duddy, just like my aunt. It doesn't fit me. Besides, who wants to read about the lives of dead people? Better to live your own life while you can."

Don had acquiesced, but he resented it when the bishop called a meeting with him and the rest of the bishopric to determine how they could *re-activate* Gloria in the church. "Why don't you ask *her*?" he had said to the three men sitting there in their suits. "*She's* the one who made up her mind not to attend anymore." They sat looking at him as if he had just told them to bugger off, which, in retrospect, he had. It gave him a little surge somewhere behind his sternum.

Eventually, he drifted away from church himself, siding with his wife's decision. There were no family obligations, no children to escort to the temple. None of his nieces and nephews, or Gloria's, for that matter, expected the strange couple who'd never had any children to show up at their weddings. That is, until he had suddenly appeared before the appropriate ecclesiastical gatekeepers to ask for a temple recommend. Don was back.

"Dirty Harry?" he asked again. "That's kind of cool!"

Earlier that day at work, Gloria had been in the back room of the frame shop and found a stash of dust-covered *Life* magazines. On top was the October 1941 issue with swarthy Clark Gable in his thin mustache and black lacquered hair imposing himself on . . . her heart seemed to stop . . . Lana Turner.

Lana Turner. How could she have forgotten the platinum blond, the flawless complexion? Good heavens, those legs! And who could forget she was originally from Idaho! She stared at the cover for several minutes. When she returned to work, she was fingering her hair. When she looked up into the plate glass window, the shop lights reflected off of it in such a way that she saw herself looking at the face of her long-dead mother. Gloria remembered the way her mother's hair "flipped" like Turner's. It occurred to her that her mother, like many in her generation, had modeled her look after the Hollywood stars'. Her mother was the Lana of Sanpete County. How could she have missed that? Why had she never put two and two together?

She recalled watching The Big Money Movie with her mother on Channel 5 where she first saw Turner in *Ziegfeld Girl* and then *Imitation of Life*, the first film she'd starred in after her daughter had fatally stabbed the film star's lover, Johnny Sompanato. There was turmoil in those smoky eyes. And that flipped hair in *The Postman Always Rings Twice*, Gloria's favorite.

Lana had died just months earlier, she remembered, the star's last appearance a horrible cameo on *Falcon Crest*. More of a scandal, in Gloria's estimation, than any stabbing. Her mother, the Lana of Sanpete County, was not a woman of scandal. In fact, Gloria remembered her mother trekking off to the temple in Manti, her little suitcase of sacred clothing in hand, where she would change into the white garb, the white shoes, the bridal veil, to save the dead by doing proxy church ordinances.

A longing rose up in Gloria. A sweet remembrance of her mother who was suddenly no longer her mother, but Lana with the legs. Lana in white. Lana with the smoky eyes. Oh, how she adored her mother! Even still, years and years later. Perhaps if Gloria had had her own children, perhaps then she would have had somewhere else besides the memory of her mother to place her affection, to posit her dreams. Instead, she seemed captive to the peripheral sight of her own Lana: Lana in the kitchen, her shirtwaist swishing at her knees. Lana in white.

Gloria had tucked the magazine into her tote bag that day. Gloria's hair was blonde, not platinum blonde like Lana's. Whose was, really? But she saw herself—and, more importantly, her mother—in that saucy flip, and hungered for more of it, for the lustful eyes of John Garfield, the itchy-footed traveler, moving over her in the kitchen of the ill-fated Twin Oaks diner outside Los Angeles.

Despite the disastrous Lulu bangs, she made love to Don that night, the first time in nearly a year. She had forgotten how strong he could be, holding her in his arms, how the tendons in his arms alternately surfaced then disappeared as he rocked and moaned above her. How tender he was as she looked into his face when he came. The way his eyes rolled back in his head. The way he sighed and smiled and even blushed at his passion when it was all over.

"I want to do the temple work for Lana Turner," said Gloria as they lay in the twisted sheet, her arm up over her head. He rose up; looked at her. "The starlet? The sweater girl?"

"She died last summer." She rolled over on her side, looking at him, a hand propping up her head. She fingered the stubble of his chin and smiled. "Lana needs saving as much as anyone, right?"

"Do you think Clark Gable has had his work done?" he asked, the idea rising in him like a bubble. "Maybe I should go through the temple for *him*!"

Gloria gave him a faux frown, then laughed. "I was hoping you'd say John Garfield. But Rhett Butler will do." Then she reached under the sheet. Don was hard again. She threw off the covers and giggled.

"What?" he said, turning red. "I *love* you!" She gripped him tightly. He moaned. She lowered her mouth to his penis but stopped an inch away from his ecstasy and looked up, sincerely —as if she were holding the mobile microphone in fast and testimony meeting.

"And I just want to say . . ." Gloria said with emotion into the head of his penis, "that I know the church is true, and that Joseph Smith was a prophet and that the Book of Mormon is true, and . . ." She fell backwards in laughter, shaking so hard she had to hold her breasts so that they wouldn't jiggle. When she looked up, however, Don was ashen-faced . . . and limp.

She stopped laughing. Don gave her a tight, consoling smile.

"I'm sorry," she said.

❧

The bishop was very happy to see Gloria. "Sister Stark, thank you for coming in. It pleases the Lord to see his children—"

"—Return to the fold? Well, here I am." She thought that the way she pursed her lips, almost a pout, was the way Lana would have done it. "Actually, Don has really set the example. He's found a lot of meaning by returning to the temple. I've noticed a change." She was saying all the right things. Both she and the bishop knew it. But it occurred to Gloria, sitting there in the bare office with the picture of the prophet and the twelve apostles—badly in need of a good mat—that she really was telling the truth. Don, in fact, *was* a new man. The last time he returned from the temple he had told her in detail how doing the work for Clint Eastwood's father had made him feel, well, like Clint Eastwood. That he sat taller in his chair at his desk. Found himself smiling in a ragged way, with squinting eyes. That Joyce, at work, had even commented admiringly on his swagger. Another time, he said that while giving the signs and tokens at the temple veil as proxy for Steve McQueen, he felt a surge of adrenaline and a sense of his future expanding before him through—yes—the eternities.

"Are you sure you weren't just re-living the car chase scene in *Bullitt*?" Gloria had ventured. She immediately regretted it.

Don was serious. The whole next week he had a smoothness to the way he moved that was right out of *The Thomas Crowne Affair*, and she found herself one night wondering how she would look with the long, black hair of McQueen's wife Ali MacGraw.

The bishop smiled warmly at Gloria. He began asking the worthiness questions—about her fidelity to her husband, her faith in Joseph Smith and the Restoration, her support of the modern-day prophet and the general authorities. Her adherence to the Word of Wisdom. As she confidently answered each of the questions, some of the old faith seemed to return. The connection she had to her mother. The abiding hope from when she was a girl graduating from Manti High that the gospel really was true. She had a testimony, didn't she? Her path was clearly marked, brilliantly lit by the detailed programs of the church she had followed . . . well, religiously. The promise of eternal marriage to a worthy man. She *did* have a testimony! The gospel *was* true! And even though the program had not worked out so well for Don and her, there was the assurance that all would be made well in the hereafter. That she would have increase through spirit children who would populate "worlds without end" through eternity.

Armed with her newly minted temple recommend, Gloria prepared to return to the House of the Lord. For three months she had attended church regularly with Don, paid her tithing, stopped drinking coffee. But most importantly, she had grown her hair out. And finally, the week of her return, she had Trudy bleach and style it.

"Ready for my close up, Mr. DeMille," Gloria chimed. The smock Trudy had just pinned around Gloria's neck rose then fell with a giant, nervous sigh. Trudy gave her a knowing look. "How does it feel to finally be doing the right thing?" she asked. She separated Gloria's hair into quadrants with plastic clips, claws bared. She had assured Gloria that the blonde hair she had inherited from her mother only needed a modest treatment to transform it into a blinding sheen. As Trudy worked over her, Gloria's excitement turned to anxiety. What if she was doing all of this for the wrong reason? Was she leading Don down the road to apostasy? She saw again her mother's face mirrored, and she realized that when her mother was her age, Gloria was a junior in high school. Did her mother dream like she did of being someone else? Even if it was just for two hours at the movies, or an afternoon of television over her ironing? The smell of peroxide began to sicken Gloria. Her scalp tingled hotly.

But Gloria's anxiety turned a corner when Trudy began styling her hair, its natural body beginning to roll and rise. She loved how her hair seemed to locate its own nuance in form, color, and light. Her anxiety turned towards Lana, or who she thought might be Lana, watching from the spirit world. Could Gloria be a worthy embodiment of Lana Turner? Would she do Lana proud? The anniversary of the celebrity's death was just two days away. She had already submitted Lana's name to the temple registrar the week before in preparation for her proxy ordinances: first baptism and then the initiatory. And now it was the holy endowment—the crowning ordinance—starring none other than Gloria.

Was she ready?

It was June 29, 1996, one year to the day that Lana Turner had expired in her Beverly Hills mansion from an unfortunate recurrence of throat cancer. And Gloria *was* ready. She took Don's hand as they walked from the parking lot to Temple Square and then through the Endowment House where they handed over their cards. The man at the counter, with spearmint breath and a practiced smile, ran their cards with great seriousness. For a moment Gloria wondered if the sentinel angels who were standing invisibly by would spitefully scramble the digital impulse that traveled to and from the sacred database of worthy Latter-day Saints. But the light blinked green. All systems go. She looked at Don, who had grown a mustache the past several weeks and just that morning had sliced away at it with his straight edge until it was pencil-lead thin. Standing there in her white dress, beige pumps, and spectacularly blonde hair, Gloria loved her husband in his black suit and tie. Loved him more than she had ever loved anything.

In the women's dressing room, she stood in her private stall, pulling the white gown over her undergarments and wishing she could wear the smart shirtwaist that swung off her hips and down to her knees: the better to honor the memory of the woman who had captured the hearts and imaginations of an entire generation of both schoolgirls *and* their mothers. (When was the last time *that* had happened?) To usher into eternity the woman who seduced and spurned the whole lot of them—not only Clark Gable but a real actor in John Garfield.

"My goal," Lana reportedly said late in life, "was to have one husband and seven children, but it turned out to be the other way around." Yes, it would be better to forgive the extravagance of a Hollywood star while dressed in the uniform she was immortalized in. But the temple *was* the temple. Modesty and tradition demanded that in this final passage of her earthly sojourn, Lana Turner's proxy be dressed as all female proxies are—as a bride.

Then Gloria saw it. For the briefest moment. A flash of platinum blonde hair, dolloped and waved, set and flipped—in the cubicle across from her. She stood stunned, watching, waiting for the woman to turn, to present herself. And then she saw another Lana Turner walking away from her toward the curtained portal where patrons are given their new name. Just the back of the woman, her hair jouncing. Gloria opened the door to her cubicle and was nearly run over by another Lana Turner headed toward the toilets, pulling at her bra strap.

"Oh, excuse me, sister!" said the Lana. Then she looked at Gloria and her face fell. She moved quickly away, not gliding on legs the color and clarity of ivory, but ambling on fat legs, rocking side to side. Gloria stood in her stocking feet, straining to see the faces of the other Lanas. The smoky eyes she imagined below a corona of white so glorious, so perfectly unreal—above that strong but perfectly contoured chin, the neck, the bust line . . . oh, dear Lord! the legs. But all the Lanas were moving away from her, busy in eternity's endless tasks, looking for the man of their dreams, the warm studio lights, the adoring eye of the camera.

Gloria returned to her cubicle and sank to the bench, her knees knocking below the temple-appropriate, satin-white dress she had married Don in so many years ago. The dress that still somehow fit her. She dropped her head to her hands and felt the old, auguring sting. The mother she loved. The mother she would never be.

She gathered up her things and fled.

Mormon Moment

❧

There is the wealth thing. As if it's a crime to be wealthy in this country, not to mention all the jobs he's created. At least that's what I think, Dot. That's what I'm thinking. But there's so much more. So much at stake."

- - -

. . . Yes? You think so? But, really, I'm not one who thinks the president is not a good man. Of course he is. A *good* man. I was so proud to see us elect a person of color . . .

- - -

Oh, Dot! No, I didn't say, "a colored man." I don't think that's how they like to be called . . . I said "a person of color." That's what some of them prefer to be called . . . It was Jaynanne . . . *uh, huh*. She said that you were uncertain, Dot. That you were being . . . yes, pressured by your son in Salt Lake. I don't mean to pry, of course. I don't . . . *uh, huh* . . . of course! Everyone's entitled to their vote, to be part of the democratic process . . .

- - -

Yes, Senator Mike Lee did say that. We're *not* a democracy. But a republic. Or a compound, compound-fractured, well . . . something-or-other, but this talk about America being a democracy, we've apparently got to stop thinking that way. The founding fathers . . .

- - -

I see . . . yes, well it is hard to forget that. Why wouldn't it be? I mean, all of those years in public schools . . .

- - -

Yes, I do think that the socialists infiltrated the schools, why wouldn't I think that? That's when bleached flour became the vogue thing, you know. In our school lunches. Scandal. White flour. White sugar."

- - -

Sandra was saying that when her daughter came back from that University of Utah there was all this talk . . . *uh, huh*. Not like at the Lord's University, you know. They have debates down there at the BYU, for sure. That's what a college education has to be about. But it's tempered by the gospel, which I think is so important in the last days. To be tempered by what the general authorities are saying . . .

- - -

The Prophet? President Hinckley? Yes, I had heard that. A Democrat. But . . . *uh, huh*. Yes. Exactly. These are not the Democrats we knew when we were growing up, Dot. They've taken such a hard swing to . . . socialism.

- - -

Harry Reid? Don't get me started. *Ha Ha!* A good man, I'm sure. And, of course, a member of the Church. But so misguided. I do like his wife. Very sweet woman. Very *good* woman. Was Relief Society president there in Vegas. Of course, he is a convert, but I'm not one of those who believes you have to be born "under the covenant" to be a good Latter-day Saint.

- - -

Oh yes. *Uh huh*. Oh, I can't imagine what Derek and Jean thought when their boy was attending, what was it . . . Reed College? That's right. Somewhere in Oregon. A nest of them up there. Yes. They convinced him not to go on his mission. Went straight to graduate school somewhere back east.

- - -

Uh, huh . . . Well, yes there is that. A terrible thing, this healthcare business, but Dot, Obamacare is *not* the answer. It's socialism . . .

- - -

Well, socialism means when the government starts taking over too much of everyday life, you know . . .

- - -

The law of consecration *is* different than that, Dot. And the Church is led by a prophet, anyway, so it is different than that. It's profoundly different, but there's so much misinformation out there. There's so much . . . yes, partisanship. I can understand why people are confused . . .

- - -

Well, I don't like it either, but the ox is in the mire. This is the moment. *Ha Ha!* Yes, the "Mormon Moment."

- - -

But seriously, Dot, and I'll only say this once to you, and then I need to get on my way—lots and lots of folks to call to get out the vote. In the end, Dot, there's only one master we can serve . . .

- - -

I do think that there are some wise parts of

Obamacare. Mitt has actually said that! Did you hear? Oh, yes! He thinks that there are some provisions that should be kept. Hooray for Mitt! I think it's very big of him. Shows real maturity. Compromise . . .

- - -

Well, yes, without compromising our values. Values are so important, Dot. And he . . .

- - -

"Yes, he certainly did. That first debate was just, well, I really felt that the Spirit was manifesting itself. And under so much pressure, can you imagine? Can you imagine what kind of—all those cameras—and. Dot . . .

- - -

Well . . . *uh, huh*, I understand your concern, Dot. But again, and you're certainly entitled to your opinion, that's what it means to be a patriot. But we would love to put you down here as a committed voter for restoring America. That's what we want to do, in the end, is to restore America to its values. Its Christian values. And strength too. We've lost so much of our influence in the world that our missionaries out there are really feeling the persecutions right now . . .

- - -

The Dayton boy. Yes. He was accosted in France. And

all he was doing was trying to defend the honor of the Church . . .

- - -

A "cult." Yes, that's what they were calling us. And fascists. And that Mitt Romney was not what the French press was referring to him as some kind of rich, out-of-touch businessman—like there's anything wrong with making a lot of money. Not to mention all of the jobs he's created. Staples is his. Yes. Did you know that? Staples is one of the . . .

- - -

Well, okay. I was hoping that I could at least offer my opinion, Dot."

- - -

I'm glad that you are not being led around by the nose. By anyone, Republicans *or* Democrats. *Ha Ha!* I've always admired your independence, which is why I've called you. Well, what I meant is this is a critical time. The ox is a metaphor. That the Jews used to describe what the priorities are for the Sabbath . . .

- - -

Yes, Mitt is so much more dedicated to Israel, of course! We are preparing for the second coming, and he knows that. He has a testimony of these things. Barack Obama does not! He's with one of those liberal sects who believe in abortions and, you know, socialism. I do hear what you're saying. And you are entitled to your opinion, of course. But Nevada *is* a swing state, as you know. And we need everyone's vote. Everyone to come out and support Mitt Romney. And the polls are showing a dead heat, Dot. A dead heat here in Nevada and, well, everywhere. We are going to win this thing. This is the moment! The news has been reporting on it . . .

- - -

Well, Glenn Beck said so, yes, but I'm sure that NPR is saying the same thing. The constitution is hanging by a thread, Dot . . .

- - -

Well, no. NPR would *never* say that. But I don't have to tell you what the prophecies are saying about that. It's Mitt Romney, Dot. He won't save the Constitution by himself, of course not. And he won't just be a puppet of the Church leadership, either. Imagine them saying that. The Brethren don't want that . . .

- - -

Yes, yes, the Republican Brethren. There are a few Democrats. You always remind me of that, *Ha Ha!* . . .

- - -

"You are right about that. But Mitt can lead out. He

can set the stage. He's got that presidential thing going on . . .

- - -

I don't know about Harry Reid, Dot. That's not what we're talking about here. We're talking about the United States of America on the brink of the greatest..."

- - -

The Stimulus didn't work! Everyone knows that. It just drove us into the economic mess that . . .

- - -

Raising taxes on the wealthy isn't going to solve that, Dot. Plus they are the job creators. You know that Dot. Your Bob is one of them. All of those jobs down at the lot are jobs that he's created through . . .

- - -

You want your taxes to go up? Yes, I know about Warren Buffett. He *is* a socialist capitalist, that's not entirely inaccurate, and he's *not* good for America . . .

- - -

I don't want to hear you mention Reid's name one more time, Dot. I mean I don't mean to be disrespectful, but you are a Latter-day Saint and you made a covenant in the temple of the Lord to support the Church . . .

- - -

Yes, okay, the *values* of the church, but also the *Church*, the kingdom of God on earth . . .

- - -

Yes, Harry made those same covenants. Yes, I know that. Apparently you're *never* going to let me forget that . . . Who can?

- - -

I don't *know* why he is so disobedient . . . Oh, Dot. I didn't mean for this to go this way. I'm so . . . just . . . certain of some things. And this is one of them. And I need to share it with you. I just want to bear my testimony to you that if Mitt Romney loses this election, and I don't think he will, I really don't, the polls are showing strong, that it really will be the eleventh hour. It will be over. Not just for the reputation of the Church of which its enemies are constantly harping on, and thereby fighting and murdering our children's faith, just ruining them. *It will be over for the country*. And I . . . know . . . that this . . . is true, Dot. I *know* that the Lord wants us to, well . . . to choose the right. That's what we need to do, and oh, how I know that the great and spacious building is attractive and the people there are beautiful, but it's the iron rod we should be holding to that will bring us true happiness. That will save the Constitution.

- - -

Hold to the rod, Dot. Hold on to Mitt's rod. And I say this heartfeltingly and In the name of Jesus Christ, Amen. . . .

- - -

Dot? Dorothy?"

City of Saints

When he arrived on the fifteenth floor of the Church Office Building in downtown Salt Lake City, Dennis Cormier's assistant alerted him that his first appointment was already waiting. The man was fleshy, jowls and hips, about Dennis's age, and carried a large manila envelope, opened and stuffed with papers. He wore a light London Fog, despite the warming weather, and a thoughtlessly tied tie. His shoes seemed to be collapsing from the inside out. Dennis invited the man in, and shut the door to his office.

"JoAnn said your name was Brother Fournier?" Dennis pronounced the name with a long "e" and no "r."

"Yes," said the man who sat without taking off his coat. "Do you know French?"

"Enough to know that folks around here probably mangle your name all the time, just like they do mine." Dennis smiled. His hesitant use of the word "folks" reminded him that he had a ways to go to acclimate to his new home. There were the words like "folks" and the single-syllable pronunciation of words like "believe" ("blieve") but also the relentless hand shaking that was almost competitive compared to Louisiana where the Church had hardly any presence. Surprisingly, Brother Fournier's hand in Dennis's had withered when they shook. And now, sitting across from his desk, the man seemed categorically out of place.

In the hall, outside the office, Lloyd arrived. Dennis could hear his mentor's voice—resonant and fresh with the office staff—as he performed his morning routine, which included waving to Dennis through the glass wall. Lloyd was a huge man with shoulders that filled elevator doors and who liked to pull you off balance when he shook hands. Dennis liked him. Lloyd was rural, from Sanpete County, one year ahead of Dennis in their three-year stint as Seventies. He could see Lloyd lumbering toward his office, looking through the Levelors and sizing up the occupants of the room, giving Dennis a querying look, then waving again.

Dennis turned toward his visitor, leaned back in his chair and asked what he could do for him. Brother Fournier turned the manila envelope over, and removed its contents to his lap. The sheaf looked like the old family group sheets which Latter-day Saints filled out with the names and dates of ancestors for their Books of Remembrance. Corners were folded, pages yellowed and punched holes ripped as though hastily taken from a binding.

"I am appealing to you," said the man as he turned over the top sheet. Dennis could see tiny square photos of blurred ancestors staring out, the look of a previous age suddenly a haunting in the room. "This is a picture of my grandmother, Eunice Hickman." The man held up a photocopy of an elderly woman with a narrow face, severe eyes and lips that thinned to nonexistent corners. The man's fingers shook. "She went by her maiden name, Fournier."

"She is a handsome woman," said Dennis, in a tepid

attempt to put the man at ease. Fournier put the picture back in his lap face down and smoothed the sheets. Dennis thought of his own genealogy, the boxes full of photos and of birth and marriage certificates. Vivian was just starting to sort through them before the accident. He had often joked that if the Brethren knew how much of his family records were in disarray they would never have called him to Salt Lake as a general authority.

"My grandmother was never allowed to take my grandfather's name," said Fournier. "At least not publicly."

"Your grandfather?"

"Jacob Hickman. You see, Elder Cormier, my grandmother was Jacob's polygamous wife. His second. A church elder known as Joseph Summerhays married them in Mexico in 1908."

Dennis looked at him puzzled. He felt there was a trap being set. "1908?"

"That is correct. *After* the second manifesto."

In 1890 the prophet had disavowed polygamy to save the Mormons from extinction. That was the only manifesto Dennis knew of, and that was all he wanted to know of the Church's polygamous past, unlike some of the locals who seemed lost in church history to the point of obsession. Prior to his ordination, in his short interview with the current prophet and president, Dennis had mentioned he was more familiar with public education than the finer points of religious history. The man, an octogenarian who always spoke in paragraphs, had reassured him. "Elder," he said, always opting for Dennis's title, "each of the Brethren has his special calling in the Church. Yours, perhaps, is still unknown to you. We don't need another church historian. We need *you*."

Dennis always figured that at some point he would feel out of his depth in his new job, even though his first year had been uneventful. When the prophet called him to be the inter-faith liaison to the region that included Salt Lake, Dennis saw the remainder of his five-year term stretch in front of him rather enjoyably.

Dennis looked at Fournier, and cleared his throat. "What is it that I can do for you, Brother?"

"Issue a formal acknowledgement."

"I don't understand . . ."

"And give my grandmother her rightful name, on the church rolls."

"With all due respect, Brother Fournier, your grandmother is dead."

"You are only as good as your ordinances," said Fournier, flinching. "What your children and grandchildren can write about you in their family histories." His jaw was set, his lips thinning like those in the picture, but through the shadow of a beard. He looked down again, spreading his fingers on the sheets of paper. Then he looked back up at Dennis. "As a member of the Second Quorum of the Seventy, surely you know that," he said.

Later that day, after the interview with Fournier, Dennis sat waiting at a table for Lloyd to get through the lunch line. Lloyd joked with the hair-netted ladies behind the counter—all of whom he knew by name—before smiling his way over to the table, his perpetually red face open with ease. He was in shirt sleeves, his suit jacket left behind, the hair on his forearms blanched from the sun, like a construction worker's. The only time Lloyd wore his jacket was when they were invited to a press conference in the lobby in front of the mural of the resurrected Christ, the skyline of ancient Jerusalem baked in the sanitized background. Dennis explained Fournier's request. Lloyd shook his head.

"What's his real beef?"

"He told me that the church has never admitted to secret marriages after the Manifesto. So he has no assurance that these 'illegal' marriages are recognized by the Lord."

"If the family doesn't believe it was a legitimate marriage, why don't they just have her sealed to her husband by proxy? It's done all the time."

"They say the original marriage was authorized by the prophet at the time. They just want it acknowledged by the church leadership now."

Lloyd stopped chewing his sandwich, swallowed hard. "Now?"

Dennis nodded.

Lloyd carefully placed his sandwich on his plate, his fingers apart, dripping dressing. "Sounds like you've gotta live one."

"They lived their lives in shame," continued Dennis, advocating for his new charge. "No one, including Sister Fournier's bishop, recognized she was a married woman. Just a single woman who kept having children."

"And this was when?" added Lloyd, finally wiping his fingers on a napkin.

"The 20s and 30s."

"And he wants some kind of public acknowledgment?"

"That this was going on, yes."

"He's going to have to take this one on faith," said Lloyd.

Dennis had hoped his colleague wouldn't say that. Dennis was young—forty-seven—and he wasn't from The Corridor, that religio-cultural stretch from Colonial Juarez Mexico through Utah and Idaho and into southern Alberta. He had made his mark as a school superintendent in New Orleans, as far as you could get from the legal world or the world of the

Big Eight (or was it now the Big Four?) accounting firms from which most of the other general authorities seemed to have been plucked. Of course, Dennis had visited the Church's headquarters regularly, as a child. He spent two months in Utah for training before he'd left on his mission to Montreal. There he was the only missionary who spoke French with a Cajun accent. Even so, he had always claimed the Gulf Coast as home, especially after the Hurricane. Katrina was the crucible, he believed, of God's necessary brutality that prepared him for what would have earlier seemed to be the pointless and thus unbearable death of his wife in a car accident. Now, he thought, he would be leaven to a church hierarchy made up of men primarily from the Great Basin and California. What Lloyd had just said about "taking things on faith," was the recurring phrase endlessly repeated in the Church Office Building when someone just didn't want to deal with something directly.

"How's your son John?" said Lloyd, diving back into his Reuben. Like everything else, eating seemed to be an athletic event for him. "How long has he been in Ireland?"

"He just got transferred to a town in the West. Lisdoonvarna. Viv and I stayed there once, actually. On our honeymoon." Dennis paused, looking down before collecting himself. "He seems to be doing okay as a missionary. Says his companion is depressed." Dennis was recalling his wife's funeral, the open casket, Viv dressed in the pleated robe over the right shoulder, the shock of green on the ritual silk apron. The putrid smell of flowers. He remembered how he had bent over the coffin to lower the veil over his beloved's face before the funeral director closed the lid.

"Those Irish Catholics can be tough," continued Lloyd.

Dennis sensed that there was something else his son wasn't telling him, something more personal and relevant than the fact that locals were not responding to the gospel. After all, that's what it meant to be a missionary. Get doors slammed in your face.

"I thought I was going to be doing ecumenical work here," Dennis complained. "Not meeting with disgruntled church members. Anyway, I told Brother Fournier that I would call him next week."

Lloyd looked at Dennis with sympathy and sighed. "Dennis, you're going to have to take this Fournier case on faith too. Don't try to reconcile the church's history with its mission today. It never turns out okay. Everyone always gets hurt." He took a stab at his macaroni salad. "Eat your lunch," he said, his fork aloft. "You're losing too much weight."

That afternoon Dennis visited the church archives downstairs. He asked for the lists of temple marriages of the early 1900s.

"Those particular records are still being digitized," explained the librarian. "I can get you the microfilm, if you'd like."

Dennis sat in front of the metal bulk of the reader, as if he were about to transgress something. He felt small. Point of fact, he *was* losing weight, the effect of running every morning in Liberty Park near his new home. At first, just getting around the park once was an adjustment because of the elevation. But now, perhaps because he had dropped ten pounds, he was winging four and five times around the wood-chipped track every day. That morning, he'd gotten a cramp in his calf. Maybe it was time to back off a little.

The librarian threaded the machine for Dennis then turned away with a courtesy that at first suggested the man and everyone else on staff knew something Dennis didn't. It was the same feeling Dennis had when he'd gone through the temple ceremonies the first time as a young man. The coded words. The secret handshakes. The knowing looks. Dennis found the date Fournier had given him in the grid, but in the lists there was no evidence of the man's grandmother being sealed in celestial matrimony to a Brother Hickman. Not in 1906.

The next morning Dennis added another lap, despite the soreness in his calf. When he had run in New Orleans and the weather had warmed in the spring—the sap beginning to flow up—he would begin to notice other people, their bodies, and feel the high-tension wires under his own skin vibrate to a distant planet. It was no different here, in "Zion," and the phenomenon, now that he was single again, both pleased and worried him. "Surely, the Lord will protect me," he said aloud to himself in a tone that sounded scriptural. He'd already been through the refiner's fire when Viv died. Didn't he deserve special protection from common, everyday sin? Just "hold fast to that which is good," he reminded himself using the stock phrase. Dennis Cormier knew what he had to do. He just had to do it. Wasn't that an asset of being a member of the restored church of Christ? To know absolutely what it was one had to do—or not do?

The cottonwood trees billowed their refuse through the summer air. The first July he had been here he had thought of the airy bits a menace, even dirty. But now he found how they pillowed on the ground, and piled against the curb, comforting. The vegetation reminded him of how many things in this dry valley were utterly improbable, the cottonwoods along with rows of planted poplars representing a personified determination of the settlers to be peculiar. Funny how he had thought of New Orleans the same way after the Hurricane and after Viv died. That other city of saints, with parishes rather than Mormon "wards." Perhaps it was time to admit that ecologically the high desert of the Rocky Mountains wasn't any more habitable than the lowlands of the Mississippi Delta, this despite the grit and persistence, historically, of their residents.

He moved off the running path to pass a slower-moving runner, a younger but much heavier man who looked like he was just starting a regimen—new shoes, a large, un-tucked T-shirt that still had the folds in it. An iPod. During his scripture study earlier that morning, Dennis had made a survey through the topical index on faith, even turning to an old commentary by the alcoholic but brilliant apostle B.H. Roberts, long-deceased. But Dennis had found no hook upon which to hang his angst. There was an air of desperation in Fournier that reminded Dennis of his days as a bishop in New Orleans and later as a mission president in California, the way some of his fellow saints saw him not so much as a counselor but as a rigid judge, one who either rules in their favor or becomes an instant enemy: "*Tell me what it is I want to hear, or I will hate you,*" they seemed to intone.

Dennis slowed to a jog at the entrance to the aviary, feeling the pull on his lungs lessen. In this post-Viv world, continually telling oneself the truth remained the most important thing. More important than belief. Than faith, maybe. It's not my job to make the past okay for Fournier, he thought. I'll just tell him to take it to the Lord. To ask in prayer and in faith for peace. But Dennis knew that was a cop out. It was what Lloyd would have told him. It was what Lloyd had told him. Surely Fournier had already done that before showing up in a general authority's office with his worn-down genealogy, pleading for understanding. Few church members would have gone that far. That's what made Brother Fournier sort of admirable, thought Dennis. What was it called, *chutzpah*?

On his way home, Dennis stood waiting for the traffic light. He could hear the train whistle to the west of the city, a plaintive cry that moved away in its Doppler slipstream. The frequent whistles had come to signify to Dennis a lingering, aural presence of Viv. And yet he realized that he now longed for something other than Viv. He could not yet put his finger on it, but it was something slowly taking form—primeval and filled with buzz. He saw the two white lines of the crosswalk before him as if they extended into morning infinity. He pressed the large, industrial-strength button for the light and waited, pulling on the waist of his now too-big sweat pants. Was it because he'd lost his appetite or that he couldn't stop running since he'd come to Utah? Now, even against this thoroughfare threading the workers into the city, the sound of the distant train presented itself as little more than background, what they used to call in movies "incidental music." And yet, the whistle penetrated him, impelling him to move on to the black top, between the lines, to cross the street against the light. Sweat beaded on his back under his shirt. He punched the button again. The light turned. The lines merged into a single, shining rod. But he just stood there.

❧

The following week Dennis picked up the phone, as he had promised, and called Fournier, but there was no answer and no voicemail to leave a message on. He was relieved.

There had been no file on Fournier from the Strengthening Church Members Committee. No signs of apostasy. No publications, nothing in the press. Fournier probably ran a small, family business somewhere in the valley, Dennis surmised. A dry cleaner or a print shop. Salt-of-the-earth type. His wife was more than likely conventional. A stay-at-home mom with several children. At church Brother Fournier probably functioned as the ward clerk, collecting tithing and keeping statistics of its members. Or he was an usher. Not exactly leadership material. Obviously, he did do his genealogy, maybe even taught the module on it once a month in the high priests quorum. Yet despite his humble, faithful service, Fournier would not be pacified by the only answer Dennis was authorized to provide.

"Only half of your problem is your job description," exclaimed Lloyd later that day. "The other half is your expectations." They were standing on the observation deck of the Church Office Building. Twenty-six stories below them, the burnished east doors of the Temple, narrow and antique, receded into block granite. South and west of them, the valley lay, alternately stitched together and ruptured by the world.

"What expectations? To be honest with this man? Help him resolve his issue?"

Lloyd turned to him. In the fierce sun he seemed exposed, the signature undergarment luminous as it pressed against his thin white dress shirt. "It's a classic top-down arrangement here, Dennis, maybe one of the last holdouts in corporate America. . . ."

Dennis could feel himself leaning away from this imposing man. "But we're a ch-church," stammered Dennis.

". . . With a prophet-president at the head," said Lloyd without missing a beat. "A CEO." They stood silent for a while, the wind wafting up the Soviet-styled skyscraper, pin-striped with cast, quartzite columns, a blinking light on top. Up here a veritable blast furnace of dry, sterile heat steadily blew. Dennis suddenly missed the messy humidity of the South.

"There's a reason why they call us 'the body of saints,'" continued Lloyd. "You get too far out there, on the tips of its fingers, and you're likely to lose perspective. The eternal perspective."

But what about one's calling, wondered Dennis. The lingering, persistent, straight-to-the-bone confirmation of the Spirit they called a "testimony"? Maybe it wasn't the world at large that needed changing anymore. Maybe it was *this* world. This valley. He recalled the prophet's words during his interview with him: *We don't need another historian, Elder Cormier.*

That night, Dennis woke to the enduring whistle of the cross-valley train. The mayor, a lapsed Mormon and cranky Democrat in, now, a thoroughly Republican world, had complained to Union Pacific that the tracks needed to be moved farther west, away from the downtown area. The persistent, shrill whistles in the dead of night disrupted the sleep of his constituents. In response, the annoyed engineers blew through the city limits, laying on the horn. Dennis perhaps alone welcomed the intrusion, as though it were Viv coming back into this world with her unfinished business, and perhaps his.

The neighborhood where Dennis lived just east of the park seemed as far from Mormon Gothic as he could get without living in Park City which truly would have raised eyebrows amongst the Brethren. He thought of Becky, his daughter. "Zion is the perfect place for you," she'd told him before he left. She was already rounding at the belly, he remembered, Josh smiling nearby. Good kid, that Josh, he thought, even if he does strike me as a little lost, still puttering around at Tulane. Was he even a junior yet?

"You've always talked about wanting to gather with the saints," Becky had told him. "And who knows? Maybe there's a sweet spirit out there working at the Visitor's Center or at the Church Office Building who you'll fall in love with." She had winked at him when she said this, and he saw the freckled girl before him, his little girl. She was too young to be a mother, he'd thought at the time. "The Brethren don't want a general authority who's a bachelor," she reminded him. The love he had for this girl now made Dennis ache.

A "sweet spirit"? he said under his breath. He thought of his secretary, JoAnn. Single. In her mid thirties. Always blushing when he smiled at her. She was beautiful, he thought, in that Anglo-Scandinavian-Utah way. But still. . . .

Dennis looked at the clock. After two. In Ireland, John would be in the middle of companionship study. He called. When his son picked up the phone, Dennis almost hung up. Even for general authorities, it was against the rules to call a missionary except on Christmas and Mother's Day. Well, he reasoned to himself, there was no Viv and no Mother's Day call, so he was justified.

"Son?"

"Oh. Hello, Dad. It's you. What time is it there?"

"Early. I couldn't sleep."

They talked about the work. The hours of walking long County Clare roads. The meeting they had with an investigator in a pub, even though it was against the rules because of the presence of alcohol. They talked about the weather. Dennis could hear his son's companion at the sink, the clinking of dishes, the sound of shoes on hardwood. Then there was a pause in the conversation.

"John, to tell you the truth, I'm not sure why I called. Is everything okay?" Another pause.

"Actually, I'm glad you called. The mission president told me yesterday I was required to call you about something. I've decided to come home, Dad. Early. Now. And I was told I had to call you. And now, here you are. On the phone."

His son told him that he'd been struggling for weeks with

the decision. That the mission had even sent him to a church counselor for an anxiety disorder.

"The counselor said something very interesting," John told his father. "But I don't think he meant it the way I took it. "He said, 'Elder Cormier, the decision is yours. You can be yourself and what you believe in or you can go on and live an empty life, devoid of all meaning.'"

Dennis swallowed hard, swiveled in his chair, pulled his robe tight around his chest.

"What about when Mom died? What about everything you said, John, before you left for Ireland?"

"I lied, Dad. I wanted to protect you. I knew you were going to Salt Lake. But . . . yes, I lied."

Dennis sat stunned, the phone pressed forcefully into his ear. He could hear his son breathing on the other end through a light static buzz.

"You can hold whatever opinions you wish in the church," said Dennis. He sounded now as if he were reading from a script. "Your faith will grow. Just give it time."

"I feel like for the first time I *have* found my faith, Dad. Mormonism may be a beautiful thing, you know. It just can't be what it has always claimed to be. And no one here wants to hear that."

His son had called the Kingdom of God "Mormonism." Dennis had understood that the work of the Lord would always be a challenge. But he had never imagined that it would be his family who would betray him. Family was supposed to be a refuge from that, a support to his work. Like Viv had been. Like Becky was—married and starting a family. Dennis had come to Church headquarters to make a difference as an outsider, even if it was just with disgruntled fellow saints like Fournier. But now his son . . . maybe at the funeral he should have insisted that John delay his mission.

Yes, his mother's death. It was too much for John. And now his son had lost his faith, his testimony that the Church was true.

"I should let you get back to your companion," said Dennis and waited for his son to respond. "I love you," Dennis said. He wanted his son to have the last word.

"I love you too, Dad," and there was a click on the other end.

Dennis sat in the dark, the traffic on 7th East a half block away almost still this time of the morning. Things were getting out of hand. He had been here just over a year, and not only had he not married, he hadn't even dated—a red flag, he was sure, in a church that enshrined marriage as its highest ordinance. And now this. John returning without honor from his mission. It was absurd. That group of dissidents, always making a stink—statements to the press, demanding an audience with the prophet, the painfully foot-noted books by "new historians"—they would find out about this: a general authority's missionary son challenging the church's truth claims, corroborating the doubts of other Latter-day Saints, validating apostasy.

"I can't help you with this, Brother Fournier," said Dennis, firmly. It was the following Monday, and he had invited Fournier back for a second interview. Dennis was in his shirt-sleeves, arms crossed at his chest, and sitting on the edge of his desk, his knee nearly touching the chair Fournier sat in. "You'll need to be satisfied with a proxy sealing in the temple to your grandfather. I'm not denying that there were men who illegally married women—your grandmother. That was a very difficult time in the church's history, as I'm sure you know."

"The prophet, Joseph F. Smith. He authorized it," responded Fournier, "secretly." Dennis was ready.

"So they say. The evidence is sketchy. Mostly hear-say. And to make a public statement that the church was wrong in not acknowledging the marriage . . . well, that can't happen."

"She was sixteen," said Fournier.

"I understand that she was young," Dennis heard himself say. Sounded like he was writing another letter to his missionary son, senatorial, conciliatory but categorically unbending. He had always tried, as he had now with Fournier, to counsel "by persuasion, by long-suffering, by gentleness and meekness, and by love unfeigned," as the scriptures said. "By kindness, and pure knowledge, which shall greatly enlarge the soul without hypocrisy, and without guile."

But then there was the scriptural counterpart that was now creeping up on him. The very next verse: "Reproving betimes with sharpness, when moved upon by the Holy Ghost." Was he being "moved upon"? Dennis wondered. Too often he fell back on his default which was that it was okay for him to think critically of the Church, but it somehow wasn't okay for others. Not in the end. Dennis could feel the hot mantle of purpose descend on him, the first time since he was set apart as a Seventy, and it felt lofty—even heady.

"You have to understand what's at stake, and, quite frankly, the covenants you made in the temple to protect the kingdom of our Heavenly Father. You need to have faith that all will be made right in the hereafter." He reached out and put his arm around the man's shoulders like Lloyd would have, to comfort him. But to Dennis it felt false. As if he were compensating for something. His own private questions? His own disobedience by not remarrying?

Brother Fournier stood. He came eye-to-eye with Dennis who was still sitting on the desk's edge. The man had moved from the picture of deep grief to a sense of calm. Surprisingly, Dennis realized that here, now, he would have preferred that the man be enraged. "My faith in the restored gospel," said Fournier, "requires that there be healing. And there can be no healing without justice." Dennis recoiled, then stood himself and placed his hands in his pockets. His slacks seemed impossibly baggy, now that he was down to 155 pounds.

Fournier turned to pick up his envelope. Despite his look of quiet resolve, the air was thick with emotion. Dennis was thankful for the sound of the buzzing, overhead light. And he was sorry. "You will get justice," intoned Dennis in his best pastoral voice, softly and with as much feeling as he could muster.

"But justice requires courage," said Fournier, then turned and walked out the door. Only then was it that Dennis remembered the man had children, and that he would be going back empty-handed to them and to his siblings, his cousins—back to his father, now ailing and who had grown up believing that he was a bastard child, a second-class saint.

Six months later and things were clearly not going as planned. John had in fact returned early from his mission and now he wasn't getting out of bed. Dennis had not even been dating, even though he had had hesitating talks with JoAnn at times when the office was quiet, and work was slow. There were whisperings going on, but no announcement from Dennis. Then there was the fact that at 5-foot-10 he was slipping below 145 pounds. Still, he kept running, even in the December slush, around the wood chip track at Liberty Park.

Shortly after Christmas Dennis received a phone call from the Assistant to the President of the Second Quorum of the

Seventy, asking him to come in for an interview. Elder D. Howard Glenn, a career general authority who was old enough to be Dennis's father, had a kind but inevitable way about him. The day of the interview, Elder Glenn was in good form, but due to his age, he also tired easily, sometimes lapsing into listlessness. Dennis waited for him to end a phone conversation about a golf game the next day in the relatively warm climate of St. George near the Nevada border. After he hung up the phone, he looked longingly at it for a few seconds before turning his attention to Dennis.

"Damn grandson. He's got a swing that will be the end of my game. Suffers a bit from too much self-confidence, if you ask me." Dennis smiled kindly at the old man. The mild profanity, he knew, was designed to put him at ease, to send the signal that this man was no ordinary servant of the Lord, that he was secure enough in his seventy-ninth year that he could present *all* of himself. Elder Glenn stood slowly, a halt in his straightening back, then crept around the desk to what the missionaries Dennis once served as President jokingly referred to as the "visiting-from-on-high chair." Dennis stood to assist him, and the man did not resist, falling back into the duplicate captain's chair with a heavy sigh.

"Since that whole prostate thing," said Elder Glenn, "I never did get my full strength back. Still . . ." he looked at Dennis carefully, and Dennis leaned in solicitously, "I'm grateful to still be here in the second estate, as much as I'd love to slip through The Veil. To move on. How are you, Elder? How's that new interfaith program going?"

Dennis began to explain the rounds he made. The deference of other faith leaders to him that made him feel uncomfortable. Their concerns about social issues, the war in Iraq. When he looked up, Elder Glenn was drifting off. He seemed to be waiting for his turn to speak, or maybe he was having a mini-revelation of the kind that the general authorities were rumored to have. Ones that often, these days, seemed to elude Dennis, especially concerning his troubled son. This time, however, instead of just continuing on, Dennis stopped. He even touched the man's sleeve. Elder Glenn looked at him and smiled. "I'm supposed to ask you why you're not married," he said. "So tell me. Why haven't you gotten remarried? Let's get this over with." Suddenly, Dennis was grateful to this man, grateful for the question, because until it had been asked in a familiar setting, he didn't know why he felt so uncomfortable about the issue. Now he did. But Elder Glenn wasn't finished. "I know you loved your wife, Vivian was her name, right? I know you are a good man, Dennis, but we need you to set the example. We don't want you to end up like Elder Mark Peterson with an outspoken divorced daughter always at his feeble arm. You may not remember that. Back in the 80s. Very embarrassing for the brethren."

"Elder Glenn," Dennis responded. "Do you remember the scripture about the body of Christ? Would you mind?" he said, pointing to the scriptures in large print on the desk.

"Please," said Elder Glenn. Dennis turned the tissue-thin pages to *Romans* and read:

For as we have many members in one body, and all members have not the same office. So we, being many, are one body in Christ, and every one members one of another.

"Paul," said the old man, nodding. Dennis then turned to the Doctrine and Covenants and read.

The keys of the kingdom of God are committed unto man on the earth, and from thence shall the gospel roll forth unto the ends of the earth. . . .

"The stone cut without hands. Yes," Elder Glenn said turning away almost as an afterthought. "The gospel will fill the whole earth. Temples will dot the land."

"That is our understanding," said Dennis, and closed the book. "But we aren't all of the same office. Our calling is to do something unique and specific to our talents."

"Which is why you were called to do ecumenical work here in Utah. We've got to start reaching out to our brothers and sisters of all faiths and lifestyles. Let them know that they need ordinances performed by the true priesthood."

"I agree with you." said Dennis, standing to return the book of scriptures to the desk. "But what that mission or calling is . . ."

"Dennis, sit down" interrupted Elder Glenn. "Now I'm not sure that I'm following you." Dennis sat. He waited for Elder Glenn to speak again.

"Dennis, you can't know what your calling is, you can't have the Lord's inspiration with you unless you are first keeping the commandments." He paused. "Your son, God bless him, needed to see his father set the example of obedience to authority. But now he's confused. Lost his testimony." For just a split second, Dennis couldn't believe what he was hearing, but then in the next moment it all snapped into place, the certainty of not only the gospel but of the terrible price of his belief in that certainty.

"You need to remarry," said Elder Glenn. "You need to remarry or we will have to release you."

❧

When Dennis returned to his office, Lloyd stood in the doorway, waiting for him. "I want you to know, Dennis," he said, "that when I first came here, I had some big ideas about how I was going to revamp the young men's program, to make it something more relevant. I admit it was disappointing when nothing I seemed to say went anywhere. But the best advice I got is what I'm going to give you. Our job is to be a soldier, not another Joseph Smith or Brigham Young. The age of prophecy of that kind is over. Our job is to obey."

Dennis looked at his friend. "I don't want to be a prophet. I just need to tell myself the truth before I can act on anything." Lloyd cleared his throat, and in that one, single gesture, Dennis felt the kinship between them drain away, and he knew that he would have to change something about himself or the rift between them would be permanent. Lloyd looked up and performed a smile and a warm, persisting hand to Dennis's diminished back.

"What do you say we go over to the Beehive House and fatten you up on some of that bread pudding?" he said. "Better still, JoAnn, she hasn't gone to lunch. Why don't you take her?"

Just then, from outside came a muted concussion of sound and a loud crack. Through the glass from the hall, JoAnn was looking at them, startled. Lloyd walked to the open door, told her to stay put, and he and Dennis moved to the elevator, but when the car finally arrived, it was nearly full, employees with worried faces. Dennis held the door while Lloyd collected JoAnn. "I will take the stairs," Dennis said to both of them as the door closed. Entering the stairwell, Dennis knew he was not going down with the rest of them. Instead, he ascended.

The observation deck was empty. The entire floor evacuated. He pushed through the glass doors on the west side and out into the cold winter air. Below, he could hear a commotion. He could see smoke. He felt alone high above the crowd that was gathering, moving with caution towards the imposing, six-spired temple. At first he couldn't see that anything was different. But he kept following the smoke. Then he saw it. The temple's heavy east doors lay slightly tilted from their frames, violating the building's perfectly ordered lines. Dennis leaned against the Plexiglas, strained to look through the smoke. He stood with his hands on the glass, fingers spread as if he were visiting an inmate at the pen and peered from this distance into the cracked frame, straining to see into the darkness behind the door. More smoke.

❧

The morning after the bombing, Dennis didn't get to the park for his run. So, later, when he returned from work, he took a long nap before waking, suiting up and then walking down to the intersection, stopping at the light to stretch in the December gloaming. He wore John's sweats, which were smaller and fit him better now that he was so thin. The rush hour traffic was over and in the park only a few runners were trailing around the path. That morning, during his executive meeting with the other seventies from his quorum, no one had said anything about the temple doors which only the city's secular newspaper had reported to have been vandalized. When he asked Lloyd about the incident as they returned to their offices, it was clear how the bombing was officially to be viewed, if it was even acknowledged. "Yes, we'll have to get those fixed, Dennis."

"But what does it mean? Do they know who did it?"

"We will have to get them fixed," repeated Lloyd, forcefully. And then: "Dennis, the Brethren do not take counsel from our fears."

Still breathless from his run, Dennis entered the house. John was sitting at the dining room table in the dark. He sat down opposite his son. John rarely left the house. The boy, now a man really, still carried his mother's face, though these days it was drawn and pale, like a black-and-white version of her in a tiny oval photo from a family history. He had Dennis's slight build but his musculature still had the taut look of feverish growth. Dennis often found himself looking at this boy with unabashed ardor that at first he thought was suspect, even carnal. But it had turned out to be something else. John was silent for a few minutes, then he spoke.

"You know how it is when new missionaries come into the field? They rely entirely on their senior companion. They would strap a bomb to their bodies if you told them to. But I knew it right away. My companion, Elder Carmichael, the one I was supposed to train? He was just like Dave."

"Your mother's brother?"

"Someone who doesn't believe. And for good reasons, not just because he was intellectually proud or, what was it someone said of him, sexually impure?"

"Your companion was struggling with doubts about the Church's claims, about polygamy and other things. That was explained to me when I talked to your mission president. Sounds as though he sowed the seeds of doubt for you?" The boy turned toward his father. In the boy's eyes lived something he recognized but could not look at directly, and Dennis finally felt the cowardice of the script he had been following like an echo—what he had been saying about his brother-in-law ever since Dave had left the church, what he had been saying about so many things. And Dennis now knew he was at risk of becoming something other than what he was destined to be.

"Elder Carmichael asked me what I thought about all the truth claims we were repeating to the Irish," continued John. "So I told him what I thought. I let him know he wasn't the only one out there with doubts about how he had been raised. What he'd been told."

"And then what happened?" asked Dennis.

"Elder Carmichael, as the senior companion, asked if I would still give him a blessing. And so I did. Even though I knew I was going to be going home early myself." Dennis was silent, a sudden aperture in the traffic of his soul. "I laid my hands upon his head and by the power of the priesthood I gave him a blessing. The Catholics believe despair is the unforgivable sin. But I think the only unforgivable sin is to dismiss someone's pain." John turned his hands palms up on the table. "To make an idol of an ideology." John looked away, out the front window, and he breathed out something old and tired, and his father marveled at his son for doing what he could not.

That night Dennis lay on the couch thinking of what he might have to do in the morning. The television was on in the other room, a program from the History Channel. He lay there somnolent, feeling alternately calm and then utterly defeated. He was dozing off when, suddenly, he opened his eyes with a start. There was a train whistle repeating itself over and over from the next room, the rising embellishments of other sounds surrounding it, the clack of metal wheels on a track. The sounds were being used as part of a score, and it occurred to him that the whistle had a meaning to it based on the music it was a part of. A meaning he could not ascertain as he was only a bystander in the other room. But he also knew that from then on, when he heard the Union Pacific whistling its way through the City of Saints that it would be only that. A train in the distance, forcing itself onwards, unable to stop.

It was then that he said his final goodbyes to Vivian, and it was like what he imagined a revelation to be. A wonder.

When Dennis arrived at work the next morning, he walked past the front of the temple. Plywood had replaced the doors while the historic, pioneer-crafted hinges, he assumed, were being re-cast. How strange, he thought. Even doors as heavy as the temple's could be unhinged with just the right placement of a relatively small explosive. In his office, he took off his coat and looked out the window at the square that had become his life and the thing he defended with all his might. Except the night before. After hearing John out, in a brief moment of weakness, he had put his hand on the strong forearm of his boy and said to him, "You are a good and faithful servant, son. Welcome home." Today, he knew he would keep defending "the Faith," but from now on it would always pain him.

It did not escape Dennis that morning that Lloyd had not tapped on the glass, had not stepped in to give him his usual good morning. He knew that what he had said to Lloyd the day of his interview with Elder Glenn had changed everything. Amazing, he thought, how simple it was to step over a line. Just one right hook to the one right place, and what had seemed implacable, huge could be dropped to its knees. "We do not take counsel from our fears," he had been told.

Seated at his desk, Dennis opened his email. There was a message from Becky about his granddaughter—one year old—and about their trip out to Utah the following week. There was a meeting schedule for the next month from JoAnn. An ad for Viagra that had gotten by the normally vigilant screeners downstairs. A newsletter advertising the latest church titles from Deseret Book. Dennis methodically clicked through all of them, deleting most, saving the one from his daughter. Then at the bottom there was one with the subject line "Justice." He hesitated before opening it. The message came from an address he did not recognize. "There can be no healing without justice," it read. "And justice takes courage."

For a split second he wished he could be his son. But when he deleted the message, he knew he would be getting married again.

Sagarmatha

As they approached the town, Eli saw what looked like a baby goat, dead in the frigid creek water, splashing down the mountain toward Lukla where they had started their sixteen-day outing. The animal's neck was twisted backwards. Ears stiff in the water. Upstream, as they crossed the footbridge into Namche Bazaar, the creek was partially dammed by a backbone of stone where it pooled. There, women washed clothes in a natural hollow, near the giant *stupa* with the almond eyes of the Buddha, trailing prayer flags. It was a place where the women could hold down the garments with their hard red hands in twelve inches of glacier water, the force of their arms keeping the *wan-ju* shirts, the pants and an occasional *chuba* from floating to the surface for air.

For Eli, the trek through the Khumbu in Nepal with his friend Clive was supposed to be a reprieve from marriage. And then, by the time Eli had arranged his flights out of Salt Lake City, a reprieve from what had turned into a separation. He was sure that by the time he got back Meagan would have the papers ready for him to sign. He stopped on the other side of the creek, physically shaking this thought from his head. Some vacation. He was here to reconnect with himself in the Himalaya, in air so thin it raked through your lungs and leadened your legs after just a few steps. He was here to see the top of the world. To test himself. He was thirty-four years old, and this excursion was going to be only about him, not Meagan. And certainly not about that incomprehensible third entity they had for three years constructed between them: a marriage, their own *stupa*.

Then Eli spied the puppy, a puff-ball of filthy, wiggling black fur—undoubtedly flea-ridden—following first one trekker, then another as it stumbled over the rocks, falling behind. When it started trailing Eli, he sped up, refusing to acknowledge it for fear of encouraging a tag-along.

❧

Namche Bazaar sat in crescent-shaped mountain slopes at an elevation of 11,400 feet, a two-day trek following the harrowing ride on a Twin Otter turboprop to the dirt air strip where Eli and Clive met Dolgé, their guide, a Sherpa with a wide face and what seemed like an even wider smile. His English was better than his compatriots', sprinkled with American expressions like "she's a hot tomato" . . . to endear him to the trekkers? Eli asked himself. What did Dolgé want in return? A shake of the head with an equally wide, conspiratorial grin? A guffaw? The first night there Dolgé had pulled out a picture of former U.S. President Jimmy Carter, his arm wrapped around Dolgé, both smiling. All those teeth—from one margin of the snapshot to the other. "Jimmee Cahta!" Dolgé pronounced, eyes bulging.

"Jimmee Cahta!" Clive repeated, stabbing at the photo with his finger. "Oh my God, Eli! Look at *that*!"

They would stay at Namche Bazaar for two nights to acclimate to the altitude, taking day hikes up and returning at night to sleep, all in anticipation of proceeding as far as base camp Mt. Everest.

All day, the pup wandered from one camp in Namche to another, a scrap of food here and there thrown its way. That first night Eli found it curled up asleep on his bag in the tent he had forgotten to zip closed. Upon witnessing this, Meagan would have been all coos and cuddles. She would have owned the situation, a regular canine savior. He thought of this briefly, then remembered the fleas, and bumped the dog out the tent flap.

The next day it rained, and the trekkers mostly stayed in the lodge where they played chess, read, and paid to take a shower before their departure the next morning. The pup was nowhere to be seen. Finally, Eli thought, a villager has taken it in, as they should. The dog is obviously homeless, he mused, an orphan barely weaned . . . if weaned.

Suddenly Dolgé was there. Beaming into Eli's face, offering him a cigarette, which he declined. "Coka! It's the *real* thing!" One of Dolge's relentless *non sequiturs*. Eli waited for Dolgé to light up. Take a first drag. Blow the smoke of his Camel out in rings as he must have seen a Westerner do. When Dolgé saw Eli watching him, he nodded, and offered him the lighted cigarette, again.

Eli pointed at an election poster, dense with script, attached to another lodge across the street. "Election?" he said to Dolgé. "What do you think of the election?" Dolgé took another drag. Even here in the mountains, the boulders and stupa shrines, the lodges and shops all had thin posters plastered to them, posters that despite their strange, scripted figures somehow embodied the same hysteria of all political campaigns everywhere. While Clive who worked as a flight attendant—a self-described "sky gypsy"—was busy taking pictures, Eli had already found something to obsess on. He wanted to know what the porters who were primarily Hindu and from the Indus Plain along with the Buddhist Sherpas thought of the election, the first free, multi-party one since 1959. In 1991, who would they be voting for?

Eli didn't expect much in response from his guide. Maybe something like "Totally awesome!" Or some lyric from Madonna, always with an exclamation point. Dolgé shrugged, the bones of his face high-pitched and hard under rich, nut-colored skin. He couldn't be any older than me, thought Eli, struck by just how impenetrable difference in another could seem. "The party communist . . ." Dolgé replied, suddenly without the clichés.

". . .Will they win?" said Eli, trying to help him out. "The communists?"

"Communist Party," Dolgé continued. Was he trying to read Eli? Figure out what Eli wanted to hear? "No. Congress Party is winner." And then, "Mark my word. BMW: The Ultimate Machine." He grinned. Eli was sorry that the Maoists or the Marxists and whatever they represented to people Dolgé called his own—might *not* win. He had taken a shine in graduate school to political theories of democratic communism. They inspired him . . . empowered him somehow. It was their clear-as-glass delineation on how power seemed to work in the world, a clarity as thrilling as the Matterhorn-styled Ama Dablam had been to him when he did a day hike the day before, and to which Dolgé, in his parade of ill-fitting, gifted North Face-branded garb, referred with a cackle as "I'm a Dumb Blond."

By late afternoon, the rain had stopped, making way for the fog that moved in waves through the town that clung to steep terrain in narrow winding streets. The fog would diminish into plumes that would rise then fall, framing and reframing the surrounding peaks of Kongde Ri, Kusum Khangaru, Thamserku and Khongeta—massifs all, like stolid giants looming above them, arms across their chests, watching. As the light waned, the pup was suddenly there again, whining and scratching at each of the tent doors. The camp finally murmured itself to sleep, but Eli lay awake. He could hear the dog outside his tent and its protests had turned to sharp, full-throated howls that reverberated through the town.

Someone ought to put that dog out of its misery, thought Eli.

Eli pulled on his shorts and his sweater against the chill, quietly so as not to wake Clive. He exited the tent, scooped up the dog, holding it at arm's length. He walked to the low-slung *gompa* down the hill where earlier he had seen two monks standing outside, urinating into the dark, the beam of their flashlights flung wildly about as they relieved themselves.

Through the doorway, he saw several of the monks sitting, their robes the color of sunlight and rust. Surely, he thought, once this helpless creature toddles into their midst, they will have compassion for it, take care of it. But after half scooting, half lobbing the pup into the circle of yellow light and the laughter coming from within, after he did that and moved away quickly, the dog turned and padded back after him. Eli chased the pup down the hill, stamping his feet in the dirt to scare it away, then returned with quick steps back to his tent.

At this elevation of nearly twelve thousand feet, he felt both winded and woozy, the blood slowly finding its way from his legs back to his head. Clive was buried in his bag, only his hair poking up in the light like spines on a sea urchin. Eli listened to Clive's gentle snoring, but he couldn't sleep himself. It wasn't long before the pup's crying began all over again, with wails pitched so high and plaintive they sent an electric current first through Eli's chest and then into his vibrating mind. And Eli was now covering his ears with his hands and recalling the last time he and Meagan battled.

"This is not your mother's marriage," he had told her emphatically. "I am not your father."

"I'm baffled by this," she said. "Elijah and Meagan reduced to just, I don't know, an arrangement of some kind." She looked at him with a kind of puzzlement that he took as contempt.

"Your expectations changed," he continued.

"Buying a house?"

"You know I'm in graduate school. And suddenly you're talking about having a child?"

"Eli . . ." she said.

"That means you'll be quitting your job."

"Going part-time," she corrected. Eli knew what that meant. *Going part-time.* It was all a ruse. First it would be, "we'll wait until you get a raise," and then "let's get pregnant and I'll keep working." Then daycare. Then it would be part-time work. Next thing you knew you were supporting a stay-at-home wife with two kids, both in diapers. No wonder his friend Darrin played so much league softball. An excuse for being gone as much as four nights a week during the season. Darrin had been hoodwinked by his wife, just like Meagan was about to hoodwink Eli. Kids, they were still the standard of modern marriage, grist for all those angst-ridden yuppies on that weekly TV series.

"I'm older than you," Meagan had said. "I'm thirty-eight. We have to make a decision or the decision will be made for us." Her eyes, set beautifully and deep in her head, were pleading.

"What happened to you?" he flared. "This is not what *we* wanted!" Meagan said nothing, but dropped to the floor with a sob. He watched her there on the floor. Finally: "I will buy a house," he conceded. "But no kids, and not until after I get my degree."

She had slept on the couch that night, he in the bedroom with his hands over his ears, like a child, to muffle her crying. In the morning he decided to take up sky gypsy friend Clive's offer for a buddy pass, fly to Seoul, then Bangkok, then Nepal to go trekking.

❧

Eli did not want to get out of his bag again. But he could not sleep within earshot of the howling dog. He needed his sleep if the next day he was to get to the next town and the world-famous monastery through some of the trail's most precipitous terrain and with the elevation climbing to a thousand feet higher than Namche. And now there was something resisting him, keeping him awake—a whiny little whelp.

All this peaceful Buddhist shit, Eli thought as he lay in the tent, *the prayer flags, and water wheels, the Buddha eyes spying on everyone. These lamas, performing for us like we're in Disneyland, blowing on their funky horns. But a tiny, helpless dog . . . they completely ignore! Now that all of us are asleep, the monks are probably watching reruns of "Kojak."*

Then, fixed in Eli's mind was the spot for drowning. To drown a dog, a puppy to be exact, is not without precedent. And yet it needs some kind of justification, a rationale. And so he sat for many minutes, peering out of the mesh window of the tent, his irritation pegging toward action. *We're here to trek*, Eli thought to himself, *not take care of a mutt. We're the tourists. Dolgé should hear about this.*

Suddenly, the crying stopped, as did the recording in Eli's head. *If that dog starts up again I'm going to have to do something.*

Eli lay in his bag, praying to five different gods that he

would not have to get up again. As he started to drift off he recalled the deep drone of the lamas' horns earlier that day, how the sound of them vibrated in his sternum down through his groin, into his legs and feet. Into the ground. He resonated with that moment even though it now somehow rattled him to think of the monks, studied, yes, but also exquisitely present. Tonight, his head was aloft somewhere, vibrating at fourteen thousand-plus feet. There was a part of him that not only needed his own way but not to be accountable for it. He found himself relying on the pup. That the dog would howl again into the night so that he would have no choice but to act.

Then it happened—the puppy's piercing cry.

Eli was up. Flashlight on. He pulled on his clothes. Meagan would surely have something to say about this, if she had been there. What he was about to do was unthinkable. Barbaric. What was that quote about a society's civility is measured by how it treats animals? The vision of her face made him hurry all the more, buckling his belt, tugging at the laces on his boots.

"Where ya goin' man?" Clive was on one elbow, his hair sticking straight up so that in the moon he looked like a child. Eli was afraid Clive who smelled of hashish would ask that question. After dinner that night, Clive had retired to the corner with a trekker from North Carolina to smoke. Back in the tent, Clive had essentially giggled himself to sleep.

"Gotta pee," Eli said. "How ya feelin'?"

"Wow, man. Is it the stuff here, or is it the altitude? I'm wrecked," and then he fell back into his bag with a snort, his arm up over his head so that the flesh on his biceps was alabaster, almost green. Clive was twenty-nine and spent a lot of time writing an extended letter to someone named Liz from his home town in Calgary and hedging his bets that he wouldn't be drug-tested by the airline for at least thirty days after his last toke. Eli waited for him to fall back to sleep.

Eli walked downhill, following the cries of the dog in the dark. He thought of the baby goat in the creek, purple in its rot. *Life obviously doesn't mean to the Nepalese what it means to us. It's not their fault.* He tagged that part of his interior script as his nod to anthropological reasoning. *The life of this dog is so far down on the list of their priorities that I am left with a decision. This dog is not my responsibility. I am a visitor. The town should be taking care of it. We spend a lot of money in a place like this. A vital part of their economy. Don't they get that?* A vision of some kind of Nepali Chamber of Commerce clattered absurdly through his brain.

The pup was easy to find on a low section of the roof of a shed near the *gompa*, crouched, rodent-like with black beads for eyes. Eli picked it up. The dog was instantly quieted, inert. But this time Eli was determined. He was not to be seduced by the fur ball with its taut, warm belly against his hand. He followed the creek past the shops and lodges, the banks of prayer wheels. He got lost. All around him was mist that seemed static and thick until, like a fleeting spirit it would rebound to a different altitude taking him in his thoughts with it.

Maybe I should relent. Go to dinner at Mom and Dad's, Meagan and I hand-in-hand. Announce we're pregnant. So much could be forgiven by that one efficient gesture! Everybody happy, especially Meagan. Maybe that's why I'm here, he thought, looking up into a shrouded sky, *so that I can get perspective on this.* But that was a lie. Despite its impressive elevation, Nepal would never be the antidote to his stuckness. Some other intractable force stymied Eli, and it originated in the West. Something equally lofty as the Himalaya but in a different way. Heady and hopelessly ungrounded: a geographically-based entitlement to live in the world but at the same time to be perpetually above it.

Above Dolge and whatever he presumed was beneath him. So tonight he was in a stage set—exotic, liminal—and he was there to act without accountability. It was his right to do so.

He found the spot. He sat facing downhill on the stone wall between the creek and the trail that one way climbed all the way to Base Camp Mt. Everest and, the other, all the way back down to Kathmandu. The sky wheeled away above him, the gurgle of water flat-lined. He looked up at the giant stupa, the flags limp now in the damp air. The eyes staring at him. Completely still, the pup breathed quietly in Eli's lap, then moved slightly.

If I do it fast, without thinking about it, I won't lose my nerve, thought Eli. He watched as another wisp of fog was borne upwards, then plunged down the trail in front of him. "Go ahead and say something," Eli said aloud to the Buddha eyes, still watching him. *Tell me what I need to know. Stop me from my deed, if you can. But don't just sit there and watch. I will climb up there and tear your eyes out of the plaster before I will allow you to sit in judgment. I was wronged. She's going to leave me, but she's going to make it look to everyone like I was the problem. She changed our story. And then she will turn the tables. Just like you are turning the tables on me, now. This dog is not my responsibility. It is an unwanted thing, and it is likely to die of starvation or sheer loneliness. I am the one left to do the right thing.*

But Eli did not move. He visualized the gesture he was once determined to make. The plunge of the pup backwards into the water. A single hand around its neck. The head pressed to the rock in the bottom of the pool, like the clothing he'd seen. The squirming. The rear paws desperately climbing up his forearm. But he would squeeze harder, forcing the issue, until the little shit resigned, then relaxed in the wake of the struggle. Until it grew cold and limp. Floated downstream like the goat.

Isn't there something about reincarnation in Buddhism? Eli inadvertently fingered the soft fur of the dog. *He'll come back, right? An eagle perhaps. (Do they have eagles here?) Or a monk, in the warm monastery watching a video of "Kojak." I am doing it a favor.*

The dog, now quieted, lay in Eli's lap completely still, one of its eyes swollen shut and oozing. More fog spirits whipped around them, and even the Buddha's eyes seemed to have clouded over, its gaze located from a more central place in the stupa. Eli slowly stood, turned uphill, holding the dog to his chest, the election posters against the rock and the building of a storefront looking like heavy-lidded eyes, yet still displaying their goods through the dark. He couldn't even hear the creek anymore. He decided he would not sign the papers when he returned to the states. And he decided that a civil war of a kind might break out in Nepal after the election, but that the people would prevail even if it wasn't exactly styled as "democracy."

Back in the tent, he placed the dog at the foot of his bag. This was enough for the animal. It hadn't emitted a peep since Eli first picked it up. Eli stroked the top of the pup's head, dislodged his boots from his feet then stood to unbuckle his belt, dropping his shorts. He climbed into bed.

❧

Six days later, Eli and Clive stood on top of Kala Patthar, overlooking the highest peak in the world with its perpetual jet streams turbulent with snow, trailing away into cobalt blue. It was cold at nineteen thousand feet, and they were bundled against the wind, dizzy with a preternatural ache somewhere deep in their skulls, legs dead to more than a couple steps at a time. When another party arrived, panting and weak, Eli had one of them take their picture, the mighty *Sagarmatha*, as they'd learned to call it using the language of their guide, as backdrop.

Days later, on the return trip, Eli and Clive re-entered Namche Bazaar. Eli saw the puppy, matted, still filthy, in the lap of a female trekker, newly arrived for her two days of acclimatization. She stroked the dog with abandon—the pup moony-eyed, content—while she threw back her head in a laugh with a fellow trekker. Boyfriend? Husband? He noticed a patch of the dog's skin showing, red with a sore. Eli turned to see Dolgé looking at him, still smiling and smiling even after these fourteen days together, as if to say, *See? We are still here. As is the dog. Again. For the first time.*

They spent the night and then returned to Lukla for the flight home, but again it began to rain. And then it rained more as they sat and waited in a lodge for five full days next to the landing strip that, when it stopped raining, was suddenly shrouded in fog with next to zero visibility. The last time Eli had heard the buzz of the Twin Otter plane was as they had descended to the trailhead in Lukla, and the need to get back to the states suddenly spiked in him.

All the way back from Sagarmatha, Eli was unnerved to hear the electioneering from radios, even as high as the town of Pheriche at 14,000-plus feet. Scores of Sherpas were trekking down and up to the voting places, men and women, in everything from traditional dress to blue jeans, some voters having flown into the mountains from overseas to cast their vote. And now this. Socked in by the monsoon, earlier this year than expected. And the ceaseless fog. There was no way to call home. Meagan was expecting him by now. Would she think he was avoiding her? That he had decided to hole-up in Kathmandu for a while? After the election, surely the country was headed down, if not the road to freedom—American style —then certainly to the road to development, to join India and

China in the rising tide of globalism, not exactly collectivism. Marxism. He could survive here. Maybe this *was* his way out of his marriage. His life. His resolve to fight the divorce that night with the pup had now ebbed, much as the persistent delirium in his head had eased out of him as he returned from the heights.

"Meagan knows we're traveling standby," Clive reminded him. "For all she knows, we just can't get out on a flight. Bangkok International is crazy this time of year." He had cut back on the hash, but was drinking more *chhyang*, the milky-white relative of beer that, at this altitude, could "knock you for a loop in a New York minute," according to Dolgé. Too many more days of waiting for the fog to lift, and they would be drinking it for breakfast. Every day a new group of trekkers arrived from up the trail and were added to the waiting list to get out. Already there was a backlog of over three hundred.

"We could always trek out," Eli said, only half seriously. "By now we could've been back in Kathmandu.

"Relax," said Clive. "You're in the Himalayas, man. Drink it up!" Clive was starting to get on his nerves. The night before, Dolgé and the other guides had gathered after dinner in the lodge, drank and danced together, a slow, soft-shoe shuffle, with steps that even Eli could have mastered had he tried. The guides were out of work until the new batch of trekkers arrived, after the rainy season. The chanting was repetitive, accented by the dancers pitching forward and making a *shushing* sound through their teeth. Now that he and Clive had ascended to nearly twenty thousand feet before returning to the airfield here to leave—Eli couldn't wait to get out of this place. He wanted a porcelain toilet to sit on, and something to eat that wasn't laced with ginger. And he was thinking about the puppy. Where it was. How it was getting on, the filthy little crying thing.

The more Dolgé drank that night, the wetter his smile became and the more stumbles and giggles emerged from the dancers. Clive had joined them, draping his arms across the shoulders of a Sherpa, one on each side. Counting out his steps, smiling away. Outside the fog reflected the lights of the other lodge uphill, but the fog was not going anywhere. Or was it? On closer inspection, it seemed to be moving, dynamic. But when a patch would clear for a moment, so that Eli could see the other side of the runway, another even thicker patch would plow in to leer at him.

He turned back toward the festivities. Dolgé was now singing, the *chhyang* from his glass slopping to the floor. Suddenly, Eli wished he could be as drunk as Dolgé was now, or Clive who was laughing in the corner, gesturing and tipping this way and that. For all Eli knew, he could be here through the entire monsoon season. What was that? Weeks? Good God!

There was a slap to Eli's back. It was Dolgé. Unlike the other Sherpas who were relatively short, Dolgé was nearly as tall as Eli, and he never wore the *chhuba* or other traditional Nepalese clothing, even tonight during a celebration of the end of the trek that was not ending . . . for Eli anyway. Come to think of it, thought Eli, no other Sherpa would have ever slapped a trekker's back like that.

"Congress Party the winner," Dolgé said. He sat and drained the last of his *chhyang*.

"Are you sure, Dolgé? They're still counting, I heard," Eli said. "The votes. Will be another week or so before they know."

"Just as Dolgé say. Congress Party the winner." He smacked his lips, and smiled, eyes drooping.

"Did you vote?" Eli asked. Dolgé looked at him oddly, like he'd just been asked if he would drown a wailing pup in the night. "You know," continued Eli. He scribbled on his hand, a check mark.

"Dolgé know what 'vote' means." He paused. Looked down.

For a minute Eli thought he was falling asleep, but then there was the forever grin breaking out again. Dolgé's grin, it was like the Himalayan sun crashing over a ridge of impossibly high terrain, a repeating moment during the past two-and-one-half weeks that always stung Eli with terror even as it eclipsed momentarily the obtuse, low-grade anxiety of his life with Meagan back in the states.

"Doesn't Dolgé care about Nepal? Its future? This is your chance to make things better for everyone." Eli could feel the falseness of his own civics lesson the moment he spoke it.

"Like a virgin. Touched for the very first time," sang the Sherpa. Now Eli smiled, broadly like Dolgé.

"Dance with us, Eli. Come dance with us," said Dolgé reaching out his hand, weather-worn and brown.

❧

"We could push you off this mountain," said Clive to Eli the next morning. "Put you out of your misery." They were lying in their bags spread on top of the spring beds provided by the lodge, their first "real" bed since the hotel in Kathmandu, the puppy lying asleep at Eli's side. It had been Dolgé who, without the men knowing it, had scooped up the dog and ported it down to Lukla. Eli had taken the fur ball immediately under his chin to obscure the fact that he was choking something back.

Clearly, the dog was sick. Panting and scratching. He had lost its appetite, and the sore on his side was large, crimson and festering and on which Eli had daubed a salve. Eli knew he could not take the dog on the plane back to Kathmandu. Nor to the states with him. As with his marriage, he didn't know what to do about the dog. Where could he leave it?

The rain was drumming on the slanted metal roof just a few feet above them. Eli had been complaining, again, convinced that the rainy season had started and that they would be trapped in the mountains now until July. He stroked the dog's back and then its belly. He had never told Clive about what he had almost done that night, sitting next to the creek. Clive had been awake when Eli returned to the tent with the pup, to sleep with its would-be assassin.

Clive was utterly familiar to Eli by now—young, chill, unattached. His friend sat up, his hair lazing and soft in the damp morning light. "I had this major fucked-up dream last night," he said, yawning. "I was trying to get to work and I couldn't find all of my uniform pieces, and I was late and shit." He hunched over, his T-shirt twisted all wrong. Finally, thought Eli, I'm not the only one here losing my mind.

"No jacket, or vest . . . something missing," continued Clive. "Can't find my flight bag. I'm at the airport, and it's like, 'if I don't get to the gate in two minutes, I'm fucked.'" He scratched his head. "And then *you're* there, man. My friend, the married Yank, hanging out with me here in Nepal. You're like in those pictures of the Madonna and Child, you know, the whole halo thing. And you're like my savior, or something in the dream. You save my ass."

Eli looked at him without expression, thinking on this. "The Madonna?" Eli said finally. "I never looked that good in blue." Clive laughed.

"Weird, huh?"

"Yeah," said Eli, returning his hand to the puppy which stirred. "Totally weird, Clive. 'Like a virgin . . . touched for the very first time'." Clive curled back into bed. Pulled the bag up over his shoulders.

"You know hash isn't legal here," he said out of nowhere. "I was wrong about that. That guy from North Carolina? He was telling me the U.S. government paid the King like forty million back in the seventies to make it *illegal*."

"Well, you're probably not going to get caught way up here," said Eli, his gaze at the pup one of unabashed ardor. "You think we get fleas from this little guy?" Clive started to laugh. His bag began to shake. In that moment, something Eli thought was critical to holding himself together lifted away from him like dancing Himalayan fog.

"What?" he said, finally smiling at himself. Infectious.

Clive rolled onto his back, still shaking from laughter, his teeth glinting. When he finally caught his breath he said, "That's what I love about you, man. I've been stoned for going on four weeks in a foreign country where communists might be taking over, and all you're worried about is getting fleas from a dog."

Eli looked at his companion, who finally quieted himself. Clive suddenly looked younger than his age, teen-aged but with a quiet torture just two inches behind his eyes. He would have to surrender the pup, which he had refused to name, to fate, just as he and Clive were surrendering to fate themselves, without actually saying it.

"Why do you smoke so much, Clive? What's the appeal? Really?" Clive looked at him, the rain pounding away above them.

"It's the only way I can stop the savage critiques of myself." Eli shook his head, giving his friend a moment.

Earlier, Eli had looked up "street dog" in his two-way Nepali dictionary and had asked Dolgé what happens to *saḍaka kukura*. He knew in Kathmandu that street dogs were everywhere, and they didn't look as though they were getting along very well.

Dolgé shook his head. "Eli, in love with *saḍaka kukura*. Not good what happen. . . . It sick."

Eli looked at his guide, the man who to Eli *was* the Khumbu, *was* Nepal.

"Poison pellets." The English word flew out of Dolgé's mouth like an arrow. Clear. Irrefutable.

"You poison street dogs?" asked Eli.

Dolgé said nothing, then ambled away, Eli's last attempted exchange with his guide.

❧

When the rain stopped and the fog lifted, they heard what should have been the welcome sound of the Twin Otter in for a landing and for what felt like a concerted evacuation of the hundreds of trekkers waiting to return to the capital city. Eli and Clive were told to pack up and be ready the next day.

Eli scooped up the dog and walked out to the edge of the village, away from the lodges and the air-strip. He was no miracle worker, despite his biblical name—either to save a marriage or a sick and abandoned dog—so he collected a plastic bag and borrowed without asking Clive's collapsible camp shovel.

The puppy licked his hand, looking up at him with his one good eye, and Eli balked at the dog's unimpeachable trust in him but kept his resolve. He wept as he walked out of sight from the others, the far-off chawing of the world's gears filling his ears before being silenced.

Flying Bishop

During a reprieve, he lies exhausted and sweating back on the bed, his T-shirt twisted at the bottom, sticking to his back. Outside the window is a single dogwood in full blossom, flooded by the high-crime outdoor lights of the hotel. When he got here earlier this afternoon for his layover, the tree caught his eye as he stood at the window and stepped out of his uniform. In the late-afternoon light, the twenty-foot tree stood in effulgent, heart-rending white—like an empty wedding gown.

Now, the tree still bathed in light at 1 a.m., Danny begins to suspect that it knows of nothing but this: that it is on perpetual display, blooming alternately under sun and street lights outside the window.

He takes comfort in this tree. From where he lies, almost the entire window is filled with the dogwood's brilliant self-presentation. Almost close enough to touch. But it's behind glass and, as in the airplane cabins where he works as a flight attendant, the windows do not open. This is what he gets tonight, this vision of a flowering tree that could bear white fruit that is sweet and purifying, even holy. Enthralled, he rises from the bed, plants his feet on the floor, stands. He walks to the window and reaches for the tree, but his hand touches only glass. And then he feels the thickening of gastric juices, the contractions, and for a moment he wonders if . . . suddenly, he is lunging for the toilet again. He heaves into the bowl, his scalp tingling with fierce heat.

He will never eat airport sushi again.

Seventeen years earlier, Danny's mother had reminded him, "Be in the world but not of the world." They were at Salt Lake International before he flew to Los Angeles for initial ground training. That was the bromide stapled to his forehead like the ruffle on the head of a hotel maid. There were more bromides where that came from: "Remember who you are," and "Change the world, don't let the world change you." He was after all a saint—Latter-day Saint, but a saint nonetheless. Even after all these years, he still made his bed before he left a hotel room. You never knew when someone might understand that you were one of the covenant people, chosen to help save the world.

"Presentation, presentation, presentation," they were told during four weeks that involved equipment familiarization, evacuation drills, first aid, food and beverage and . . . Kayla, who asked him every day as they walked across the street from the dorm to the training center if this was his last day. She was feeling as ambivalent as he about the "safest way to travel," and both had talked about bolting. But, what the heck. The job was a one-year hiatus before graduate school—that's what Danny told himself. And then it was back to Utah where his life—"the" life—would start in dead (and deadening) earnest.

"Last day for *you?*" he would say, repeating the question back to her.

"I like the rampies in uniform," she said on one occasion, eyeing a tug as it rounded the corner of the G.O., its driver in shorts. "Cute asses. I think I'll stick around for a few more days." She smiled, the lipstick at the corners of her mouth smudged out, and her eyes disappeared into slits behind her sunglasses. Out of all the other flight attendants in their 1985 class, he had become friends with a Long Island Jew the height and weight of a Russian gymnast. Why not the young women from Utah where the airline was hiring for their new hub in Salt Lake? Why not the seven other men, most of whom seemed inordinately concerned about using the right shade of bronzer for their appearance checks? Instead it was Kayla the Jewess.

"It's the persecution complex," she said, weighing in on the why of their attraction to each other. They were in a hanger doing evac drills off the 727. "Of course we lost six million. You guys have a ways to catch up." They were standing next in line to take the jump on the door slide, yellow and obscenely tumescent, the group giddy in their jumpsuits. "Maybe if you started wearing yarmulkes. Something more distinctive than the fact that all of you look like your first name is Bjorn and like none of you have ever had sex." With that she stepped up to the lip of the 1L door, her arms straight out in front like Olga Korbut, and jumped.

Kayla had been living in Los Angeles long enough to have dated a couple of Mormons. She had even been to the ward once, she explained to Danny, and bought a lace dress and white pumps with tiny white bows for the occasion. Her effort at cultural assimilation.

The night of their graduation, Christian, one of the other trainees, started rubbing Danny's leg under the table so that he nearly spilled his cranberry juice. Kayla interceded. She pulled Christian's ear down to her mouth and whispered something so that when he hoisted himself up to go back to the bar he looked suddenly sober, a red smudge on the lower lobe of his ear. Then she told Danny they were evacuating. "Release seat belts! Get up! Get out!" she giggled, using the commands they had learned during drills. "Leave everything! Good exit! Come this way!"

Back in her room, while she was in the bathroom, he sat on the bed and felt the same curious wave of untethered desire move through him that he had felt when Christian had rubbed his leg. A kind of larceny that was free-floating, unattached. Not like the low-grade buzz of being in a bar—even if he was only drinking juice. This was another first for him. Alone with a woman in her room. And this foray into Gentile ways seemed truly dangerous, but delicious. Danny was a twenty-five year old virgin because sex outside of marriage was the sin next to murder. *If I can just make it through training*, he thought to himself.

Suddenly, Kayla was standing in front of him, a wisp of a woman in an open-throated, oversized dress shirt over something black and fixing an earring. When she dropped her hands, it glinted silver behind her dark curls. Everyone had been given their domiciles earlier that day. Danny was headed back to Salt Lake and the new hub there. Kayla had elected to stay in LA. "You know you're the only straight guy in the class," she said, turning toward a mirror and re-applying lipstick.

Danny answered. "That's what Christian says. But he thinks every man is gay deep down."

"Every man's *a man*," said Kayla, turning around. She smiled. "Little Christian may be just one more stewardess trapped in a man's body, but he is still a man first." She sat next to him, her perfume stinging the air. The Sunday before, their one day of the week off, Kayla had convinced him to skip services at a nearby ward house and go to Redondo Beach with some of the others where she drank tequila straight and danced to R.E.M. on her walkman. *Be in the world* . . . That afternoon Danny told her he was a virgin . . . *but not* of *the world.*

Now, on the night of their graduation, she made her own confession. "When we first got here, I thought I was going to have to bop you," she told him. Danny wasn't flattered. He was annoyed to think he was someone Kayla—obviously not a believer—imagined she could simply set her sights on, and have. And yet her impulsiveness was what he liked about her. The way she had blown out of New York to California with no job prospects just because she fancied herself a surfer, or someone who dated a surfer. The way she danced in the sand at the beach, her arms swaying above her head, her eyes closed, the perpetual red-lipped smile. How her Jewish-ness was about who she was, and not what she necessarily did. In Danny's mind, it was also about what she didn't do. One of the not-so-chosen people anymore.

He felt a sudden spike of self-righteousness and remembered how on his mission, a two-year proselytizing tour of the Carolinas, he had the sense of God's Kingdom being a mighty ship, steaming steadfastly through the dark ocean of night, moving stolidly toward a glorious and sure destiny. The Kingdom had always been just the tacit web in which he lay suspended until one night at scout camp in the Uintas when he had felt the Spirit and had a conversion experience; the scoutmaster bearing testimony around a campfire of Christ's restored church in these latter days before the troop knelt in prayer to close out the day. The stars wheeled above Bald Mountain, the whole scene a curious, unexpected imprimatur of faith now on his heart. Later he lay in the open-faced cabin and thought of his father whom he had never known, mysteriously gone by the time Danny was age five. The wind pounded at the pines surrounding him, but he felt not only at peace, secure within the tribe of believers, but impelled to be the servant of that tribe and to the broader world at large. A missionary.

But upon his release to return home from his full-time church service in North Carolina, the path had become unclear, or undesirable, which was arguably the same thing for him. Why, he asked himself, didn't he get married like most everyone else did before he graduated from BYU? If he had married and the children had started to come, everything would still be clear, but now he was in a dorm room with a beautiful woman who had just told him she wanted to fuck him as some kind of lark.

"But if I can't have you, Christian can't either," she said.

"I'm flattered."

"Are you? I've come to think of you as asexual."

"Thanks a lot."

". . . and someone who is truly good."

"I try hard." As he said this he wondered if it sounded like the sin of false modesty. He'd always held to a premium keeping up appearances for the cause, to be an example to others, a reflection of the Truth he felt compelled to embody. He was the golden boy, the darling deacon, always being tapped to lead the other boys in scouts and in the priesthood program. And when he faltered and was questioned about his involvement in incidents of mutual masturbation, or when obedience simply did not produce the expected results, Danny recalibrated his performance to ensure that other's trust in the system remained intact. That the covenant people were indubitably in the world but not *of the world*. Set apart.

Kayla touched his hand. "I'll miss you, my little Mormon mensch. This place needs you. But don't forget that maybe you need it." Danny wasn't sure what she had meant by "this place."

"I shouldn't have to apologize for my standards," he said, defensively. "Not everyone can just drift around in passing pleasure." He was starting to sound like his mother.

"Always striving, aren't you?" Kayla sighed. "At least you're smart. At least I don't have to worry about you becoming one of these flight attendants who only reads *People* magazine on the jump seat." She had called him smart. She had called him asexual. Danny would only remember that Kayla had called him good, truly good.

❧

After a year in Salt Lake base, Danny cut back on his hours and started graduate school, but withdrew soon after. There was something too final about school, as if it were a flight leading into the celestial blue that once on, he would never be able to get off. In 1987 he drifted into a gym one day, eventually transformed his body with thirty pounds of muscle added to his frame.

Every few months Kayla would call him. And on his layovers in Los Angeles she would pick him up at his hotel and drive to Venice Beach where they would dodge the bicycles and in-line skaters, negotiate the indigent. Despite the California sun, Kayla's skin remained the color of ivory. Even in a light chemise, she had that dressed-up look New Yorkers never seem able to shed. Under her arm she carried a large black bag, rectangular, the handles looped over her shoulder so that it looked like a giant portfolio. And when she stopped to retrieve lipstick, a mint, or one of several paperback books, her eyes would squint as she peered in before she seemed to plunge into its maw, her arms flailing in and out of the vast clutter.

At Muscle Beach they sat eating frozen yogurt and watching the bodybuilders pound iron on the outdoor weight pad. To Danny, the men were not the freaks that some made them out to be, but beautiful, exotic animals. What fascinated him was the systematic rotation of myriad parts that were built and shaped by the intense training. The program of sets and repetitions for the broad plates of the pectorals so close to the source of engorging blood as compared to the dense, stubborn calf muscles at the most distant outpost from the heart. It was the subcutaneous experience of getting a "pump" in your muscles; how it made you feel. It was the sex as much as the science of it. These men were both human but decidedly unreal. A vascular version of Kayla's "truly good."

"One squeeze from one of those guys, and it would all be over," said a transfixed Kayla from behind her yogurt.

It was the first year of the new millennium and he needed a change, so Danny transferred to New York City to work international rotations and maybe try once more to go back to school, and perhaps even find someone to marry. Marriage, after all, was a requirement for the highest heaven. Danny even started drinking coffee, contraband in the faith along with booze and tobacco, but something he liked to take in a stack of pre-workout supplements every day before hitting the gym.

"Steve Young isn't married," Danny reminded his mother on a trip home. "And he's the Mormon poster boy."

"Steve Young plays football for the 49ers and probably sings bass in the ward choir. You're a flight attendant and a tenor with six sisters and you probably haven't been to church in over a decade."

Danny preferred to think of himself as a baritone, but his mother was right; he hadn't been to the ward, let alone the temple, in nearly twelve years. He had even missed the weddings of his two youngest sisters, not because he couldn't get off work, as he told them, but because he wasn't able to obtain a temple "recommend" from his bishop to attend. The truth was he didn't even know who his bishop was, or what ward he belonged to.

One September morning, in his second year in the new domicile, Danny got a phone call from Kayla. He had spent the previous night trying to beat back a fever, but now he was feeling rested. Kayla had transferred to New York herself six months earlier, but he hadn't even seen her.

"Last day for you?" said the voice on the other end. He smiled.

"No, I like the asses on these rampies," he joked. "I think I'm going to stick around for a few more days." He imagined Kayla walking along in black boots, a smart-aleck smile, cell phone to her ear, the lipstick in the corners of her mouth rubbed out.

"Byron and I split."

"I heard. Through the grapevine."

"Doctors are going through too much of an identity crisis these days. They feel underappreciated or something. And then they have to pay all that malpractice, anyway. It got old. Of course there was the little thing on the side he had going with Nurse Fucking Ratched."

"What are you flying these days?"

"I try to stay out west. Trans-con to LA mostly. You know, Danny, I don't care if my people are complete pains-in-the-ass going from LaGuardia to West Palm all the time. I think a lot of flight attendants are just anti-Semitic."

"Your dad would be happy to hear you say that, you know. Defending your people."

"I would never tell him. He'd just take it as a sign that I was going back to temple and giving up prosciutto. I had to prepare the cabin yesterday."

"You're shittin' me?"

"Landing gear wouldn't go down. I'm standing there in the aisle with this hangover trying to show everyone how to brace, and I feel like I'm going to throw up on top of this man's head. And he was already wearing a toupee."

On Kayla's flight the landing gear had gone down. It was the indicator light in the flight deck that had malfunctioned. Even so, she said, she would never forget how everyone on that plane suddenly loved her exquisitely for just that ten minutes before they landed safely.

The two of them had lunch. They spent the day walking in Riverside Park and sat on a bench watching the sun set over the Hudson. Kayla had become more and more petite over the years, her upper arms so thin and so white, he imagined they could break in two with a snap. He often teased her that if Orville Redenbacher's and TCBY went out of business she would starve to death. At recurrent training the year before, while being tested in automatic door operation of the 757, she had hung onto the wrong handle and gone flying out with the door when it opened with a pneumatic lurch. Fortunately, the drill was in a mock up.

Next to Kayla, he felt huge and ungainly in his studio physique. It was like when he had layovers in Peru, and he would walk the streets of Lima, his size and shape pressed in hard angles against his thin cotton tee, and he seemed ludicrous in this world filled with the hardscrabble commerce of men and women whose bodies were the natural consequence of their lives.

"There's just one thing I can't figure out," Kayla said.

"Just one?"

"How do you divorce the father of a child you've become the mother of?"

"You really took a shine to Brandon?"

"He needs me. When he came to live with us after that god-awful military school his mother sent him to, it was like he was living in another country and it took a full year to coax him home. And now . . . " Kayla turned away, in a failed attempt to collect herself. Danny was silent, the contrails of a jet high above them suddenly taking his focus. "And now, I know that I need Brandon as much as he ever needed me."

He waited for her to explain.

"I need him so that I can know what I'm capable of. What kind of person I can become."

"Are you still in contact with him?" Danny ventured. He felt as if he were a Mormon bishop conducting a worthiness interview for a temple recommend and had to struggle to appear empathetic, and he thought he could hate himself for that one thing. The performance of that one thing.

"It will never be the same. And you know what? It was a tender event, saying goodbye to Brandy. Sweet really. Not like it was when I left New York. Left home. Sometimes I cry when I think of you, Danny, my little Mormon mensch. I used to think you were like this Arab in white—the exotic 'other'—riding out of the hot desert, clean and innocent. But now I realize I'm just crying for myself. For something I've lost. That the world is too much with us, like someone said. Are you still immune from everything, Danny? Like you were in LA? I suppose I've idealized you over the years."

"It's my pecs, isn't it?" Always ready with a pithy remark

when she talked this way. But it was indicative of what he had come to need. To be thought of as somehow superior, more righteous, more innocent—more muscular for God's sake—than everyone else.

"I always liked a man's back more than his chest. Something about that V-thing going on . . . sends me somewhere. Makes me want to bop him."

"I'll remember to keep my shirt on. Wouldn't want to ruin a good friendship." In fact, at that moment, he would have risked friendship and more to take Kayla back to his apartment and make love to her as he had sometimes fantasized. But that couldn't happen. Especially not that week. His desire for her began to pale, and he had the impulse instead to tell her why he loved her. That she embodied something he could never have. The sum of one's parts. But he didn't. To do so would threaten the only spell he felt he could cast on anyone, even on his best friend.

"I am sorry about Brandy," he said, finally securing the line in his script. She leaned against his sculpted shoulder, hard as alabaster, and he slid next to her.

❧

In "Babylon," the term Danny's mother used for New York City, Danny had been learning that it was men, not women who appreciated arms as hard as alabaster. He noticed he had the attention of what seemed like every man when he went running on his off-day from the gym. He remembered it this way: one day he was running in Central Park when he saw a man walking out of the bushes near the great lawn. He was zipping up his pants. Danny finished his run, but the next day, after lunch, he made a short-cut through the park near where he had seen the man. It was late June, already warm and humid, and the trees were fully leafed-in and dense. Through the foliage were trails, and behind a bush, resplendent with honeysuckle, stood a man, and behind a maple, another, smoking, his other hand almost imperceptibly rubbing his crotch. The second man stared blankly at Danny, moved to the tree trunk where he stubbed out his smoke, turned to look at him again, then disappeared down a trail.

Danny followed him, and the old feeling of disjointed desire he had felt from time to time reappeared in him like the dappled sun through treetops, the same response he sometimes had in the locker room at the gym, on the hot summer streets of Manhattan, next to Christian on graduation night from training and in Kayla's dorm room afterwards.

But this time, the object of desire was himself. And once the man he was following knelt in the leaves and savagely took Danny's cock in his mouth, Danny felt as tall as the trees, and as big as Central Park and he found himself taking off his shirt so that the man could worship him unencumbered.

When it was over, Danny felt sick. He knelt in the dirt and vomited. It was the memory of the sound of the man breathing and slurping against his balls, the smell of tobacco. The grip of the man's hands on his chest, the feel of the man's wet head in Danny's hands. But more than feeling sick, he thought of Kayla. How if she only knew what he was capable of now.

He went back to the park again after his next trip. And soon it was every two weeks or so. Each time, at the moment of climax, he became instantly repulsed by the man who had serviced him, and he would stumble to get his shorts pulled up and be on his way. But every time he returned, it was as if the Mormon Tabernacle Choir were lifting the tops off the trees with the *Battle Hymn of the Republic*, and he felt strangely at ease in this temple of charged desire.

Once as he entered his sanctuary, intent on getting off, he came upon a man in a wheelchair. Somehow the man, who was about Danny's age, had pushed his chair off the sidewalk, into the trees, onto the trail and into a stand of saplings where he sat fingering himself. The man looked up at Danny with an almost hopeless pleading, but Danny, disgusted, fled the scene. Later, he would return to that spot, and finish the great work that burned him from the inside out. The man in the wheelchair was gone, but Danny found someone else, and in the throes of passion he imagined the sound of a wheelchair creaking as he straddled the paraplegic, whose arms made powerful from pushing himself through life, wrapped around Danny's waist. Revulsion at the thought did nothing to keep him out of the woods.

On a layover in Manchester, England, a burning in his urethra began whenever he peed. When Kayla next called, he was still on medication for gonorrhea. And there were still occasional fevers, and he wondered for the first time, now as they sat on the bench overlooking the Hudson at sunset, if what he had done in the park not only prevented him from sleeping with her, but compromised his capacity to minister to her. After all, he was still one of the covenant people. The truly good. And the chosen were to minister to a sin-sick world. If the face he had fronted to her—and arguably to himself—was false, was he unworthy to be of service as he was destined to be? That was Utah think, he decided. Kayla wouldn't give a shit what he was doing in the park. It wasn't like he was hurting her. Still, the thought of telling her . . . no, he wouldn't do that. The park was the one place that he could still feel bigger than life, as if he were being lifted off the ground in theophany. It was too important to risk condemnation from anyone. He was thirty-eight. The park was the only place where he felt alive and most importantly, weirdly perhaps, it was the only place where he suspected that he was not as innocent or "good" as Kayla claimed.

❧

Back on the bench overlooking the Hudson, Kayla shifted against Danny's arm. "How's your dad?" he asked her. She thought for a moment.

"He told me last week he could live with the fact that I don't even observe the high holidays. And the fact that I refused to marry Jewish. He actually liked Byron."

"And what is it he can't live with?" Danny asked as a jogger went puffing by. For a moment, Danny wondered if the jogger ever found himself in the thick trees of Central Park.

"That I'm anti-Jewish. That I fight it."

"Judaism?"

"One little remark about Sharon's killing the Palestinians and. . . . Life is a complicated, exasperating thing," she said. "It's not just about taking sides, it's about holding all of what you can of it and then acting anyway, with hope." Suddenly she looked worn-down to Danny. Older. As if her time with Byron had peeled back any semblance of a veneer to reveal the price Kayla was paying to live a life which started with her daring move west and led to becoming a surrogate mother. He wanted to believe that Kayla could be Kayla without what he perceived as negative residue. That like him she could traverse the whole world, love and be loved, then leap unchanged back into her former self.

"Do you have any regrets?" Danny finally asked her. Kayla lifted her head and pulled her sweater closer around her. He could tell that tomorrow would be even more beautiful than today by something in the air, a stillness in the city that reminded him of that moment in an airplane, just before it begins its gradual descent, when it seems to dangle at the apex of what is little more than a parabolic arc drawn in the sky—a giant arc from point A to point B.

"No regrets," she said. "Just wonder."

"Like when you were a kid?"

"Before I moved back here to Long Island, I used to always go on extended walks in the morning when I laid over here. I guess it's sort of a ritual. And now to do it, it's almost more than I can bear. I'm amazed things work in this world as well as they do. It's truly a wonder. And to think that I've been a participant in all of this." She looked at him, pursing her lips. "I regret not coming home earlier. This place is my home. It used to be the place that owed me something. But now it's the place I owe something to. I feel like I need to rescue the world like it has rescued me."

"The world has rescued you?"

"I loved my husband, Danny. And even though it didn't work out, and I feel . . . I am devastated by all of this. I'm glad to be here but glad that I've been 'there.' To love well has been its own reward." She was crying now. Sniffling into the breeze. But Danny could only feel himself floating away on it.

"And not sleeping with you," she added after a while. "I also regret that. Not the bop. But actually sleeping next to you. There would have been something comforting about lying next to someone like you who still seems to hold to an ideal at any cost." Danny thought about the cost, the secret disease of it, and then he invited her to spend the night at his place.

As they walked back to his apartment on the west side he said, "I have an early report tomorrow at Newark. Stupid turn is all. But I couldn't get rid of it."

"By the time you're up, I'll be halfway to Battery Park in my new Reeboks," she said.

At the apartment Danny took his ciprofloxacin then

climbed into bed with Kayla where they lay holding each other through the night. Outside, Babylon seemed still, and it was still—a fragrant promise of urban canyons to be filled again with sun in the morning. And Kayla smelled like the sweet decay of sorb-apples at the end of an English summer.

❧

When he awoke, she was gone. Danny hurried to dress, then decided to splurge and call a car service. At Newark, he casually threw his bags on the conveyer belt and nodded to a yawning young man looking at the X-ray screen. Danny remembered the night before and the memory of what he was capable of burned within. The night before he had had unprotected sex with Kayla. This while he still suffered from the late stages of a sexually transmitted disease. This while he waited for his HIV test to come back.

Sitting on the jump seat, waiting for takeoff, the familiar burning began to subside. In his mind's eye, it wasn't Kayla he saw, lying betrayed by him in his bed. It was his chiseled self, asleep, on the edge of a dream. Innocent. Immune. One of the chosen. He could fly.

He stood in the aisle of the 757 and watched the passengers trundle in, displacing with their heat the emptiness of this narrow-bodied world. There was no place for him in this aluminum O. He could only be a facilitator to life, a kind of pastor, a sort of judge—one who serves drinks to those going somewhere, while he himself would always just be en route.

When they landed, the captain's voice came on the PA and asked for everyone's attention. He said that all flights had been grounded, and that anyone making a connection would need to talk to a gate agent inside the terminal. Then his voice cracked, and he said, "The nation will never be the same after this September morning."

❧

Danny wakes. The dogwood outside his window is ablaze in morning light. He looks at the clock radio. Nearly seven. He's slept four hours and is feeling much better, though his sides ache. The bedspread lies on the floor, crumpled, the smell of vomit still heavy in the air. He lies on his side, his back to the window. He thinks about the tree. He never noticed it eight months earlier when he was stuck in the same hotel and, coincidentally, the same room, for four days following the attacks on New York. Of course, the tree wasn't in bloom in September as it is now, and back then he was fixed on the television like everyone was, watching the city that he lived in on a screen, as if it were being beamed in from another world. He had called Kayla's cell phone seven times that September day, leaving messages. Then he called his answering machine to see if she had left a message. After that, he had called her cell just to hear her voice.

"Hi. I've missed you. Please leave a message and I'll call you back."

He has three hours before he has to be downstairs for report. He can do it. He can get up, shower, put on his fire-retardant uniform and play his part to keep the industry aloft. Since 9/11 he hasn't balked at going back to work. In fact he volunteered during the following weeks to work with the trauma counselors at the New York domicile. Three hours and Kayla's image appears to him again, and again over the beverage cart, standing in the aisle of a busy flight. She is wearing her lace dress and the shoes with tiny bows on them, but she is laughing. Danny turns toward the hotel window and the dogwood, decadent in this brief yellow moment and bruised by the wind. The purging has left him feeling light. "Last day for you?" Kayla asks him, warmly.

Even when his mother pleaded with him at Christmas to transfer back to Salt Lake, he was resolute in a way he has never been since he was a missionary knocking on doors in Raleigh and Fayettville, peddling religion.

At work now he thinks of crashing all the time, as if aviation has finally called its own bluff and admitted to the Icarian fantasy that flying has always been. On gradual descent, when the engines cut and the nose falls ever so slightly, he still knows what the drill is. But he also knows that this one is failing, like every drill he's ever put himself through, every belief he's held. And yet this vibrating tube still holds the world as he has come to know it, and in this world he is its bishop. He feels protective of this clutch of strangers assigned to him, as if his heart will break for their expectations of life. And so, despite the fear of dying, there are molded plastic smiles all around to reassure his charges who, every time there's a bump, look at him as if they love him exquisitely.

"People need me," he'd said over Christmas break to his mother and sisters with worrying faces. But really what he meant, but could not say was, "I need the world."

"I belong there," he said, referring to Babylon. His mother looked at him, standing before her in his armor.

"Your father could be brave," his mother said, reaching up and cupping his face with her hand. "You got that from him, you know. You know that, right?"

PART III

HELLO AGAIN, FOR THE FIRST TIME

Angels in Utah

A FLOOD FANTASIA ON MORMON THEMES

with apologies to Tony Kushner

Below Ensign Peak sits Y. Rex Hyrum Callister Fielding Jorgensen, who by name alone is a blueblood. He sits atop a giant boulder, half a bag of chewed sunflower seed husks littered about him, binoculars to his eyes. He is focused on a house below him and the cherry red pick-up backing out of an arced driveway, the white brick house framed by scrub oak, the back of the house stepping precariously down the hill into a second level. The pick-up waits for a passing car—the occupant of which honks and waves—then bumps out into the empty street facing nothing but the muddy mountain, the same mountain upon which Rex, thoughtfully cracking seeds, is perched. The pick-up slowly moves down the street, then down the hill to the city of symmetry ringed by violent, white-capped peaks. Rex holds his breath, a single seed wedged seam-side up between molars.

Six years ago, when he was eighteen, Rex broke into a gas

station late one August night. As he sat in the office chair looking at the stapler on the desk and the wall calendar of scantily-clad women weighing down the hoods of cars, a certain euphoria came over him, a steady current of adrenalin that brought him enormous psychic relief. The same relief he hungers for now.

Rex watches as the front door of the house opens, and a young woman, holding a crying child on her hip, pads out in bare feet to pick up the newspaper. At the open door, another child, a twin, in nothing but a diaper, crawls into view, eyes wide. Through binoculars, Rex can actually see the dimples on the back of the crawling baby's hands. Resolved, he bites down on the salted seed, his tongue expertly fishing for the meat. Tomorrow, on Sunday, this family will be in church at a ward house less than a five-minute walk away. They will not bother to lock their door in the safe neighborhood known as the Upper Avenues, and this residence framed in scrub oak will become the Sunday School Burglar's third hit of the day.

❧

Now it is April, 1983, and the shifting, water-logged mountains have opened their veins with a groan. Blood spills down their flanks in aspirating heaves, carrying trees and boulders, trucks and abandoned après-ski cabins. With their flinty tops these mountains are considered young, but they feel older than their years. The suspense of straddling a fault line threatening to slip has made them feel tired, worn, more Appalachian than Rocky. And now record snows, heavier-than-usual spring rains and finally, fierce, high-desert heat, crumple the glaciers into raging, exfoliating currents.

But something other than the dissolute mountain range's need to purge is demanding a hearing. Something civic. It is the blood of the valley people that is crying out, blood that is blue, soulless—not yet alive. Blood that needs to become red.

❧

S. Einar Hinckley Packer Leavitt Allred, also a blueblood, carries a multi-segmented name that dates back to the time of the pioneers—of the English and Norwegian stripe—and today, he is sitting in the cab of his cherry red truck, waiting for the traffic light at North Temple and State in Salt Lake City. For days now, people have been sloshing through the intersection in the overflow from City Creek. Across the street rises the mighty Church Office Building, anchored as it is on a double-winged base, each side displaying an earth orb in bas-relief—stone testicles to the tower above. The sight of this building always makes Paul feel inadequate, but he has not told anyone that, certainly not his blueblood wife, Donna Catherine Eliza Pratt Allred, home with the twins.

The light turns green, and Einar moves slowly into the intersection, the water hissing at his tires. Along the north side of the street, scores of tiny ministering angels are piling up. Eight inches tall and referred by acronym as "M.A."s they have been fixtures in the city since the 60s when the Great Work of saving the dead was significantly stepped-up. Now they are everywhere in the city, unable to get their wingless, poochy-faced selves and their endless piles of names, extracted from old histories and records, across even three inches of water. Heavy laden, the M.A.s are headed past the Church Office Building and to the temple where the names will be added to the great lists of the dead who still need to be baptized by proxy.

Einar considers stopping for a moment to ferry the M.A.s across in the back of his truck, but there are too many, and he's not particularly fond of them anyway. Too self-important. First one—his robe caught under the foot of another—starts to fret and then another lets out a cry as he inadvertently gets pushed off the crowded curb and into the gutter, gushing with water and leaves, sticks and small stones, water headed for the already flooded storm drains. Some of the extracted names float in the street like leaves: Thomas Germaine Miller, Susan DeBry, Benjamin Dubno. A speed bump in the Great Work, Einar thinks. That's all this is. Nothing can stop the work of the M.A.s, immortal cherubim that they are. Einar decides they can take care of themselves. Besides, as a collective they only make him feel guilty.

From North Temple Street, Einar heads up Emigration Canyon to higher ground where he stops at Ruth's Diner for coffee. The sun is blazing like July, three months early, and the plate glass of Ruth's ricochets light. The sky is cloudless, and behind the diner he can hear the roar of what is normally a babbling creek. This year the creek, frenzied as a high school cheerleader, is swollen, rushing down the canyon on its way to enter the exit-less Great Salt Lake.

Inside the diner, Bishop D. David Mitchell sits at the counter, reading *The Salt Lake Tribune*. Upon seeing the back of the bishop's head with its signature bald spot the shape of the African continent, Einar does a military one-eighty and heads back out. Can't be ordering contraband coffee in front of his bishop, he is thinking. But Bishop Mitchell sees Einar before he can leave.

"What a pleasant surprise, Brother Allred," says the bishop with a limp grin. "Didn't think I would have the pleasure of interviewing *you* over breakfast." There is no such thing as a conversation with one's bishop. Only an interview, even (especially) when it is masked as a conversation. Einar considers that at least Bishop Mitchell doesn't pretend otherwise. The bishop pats the stool next to him. "Quite the spring we're having." Einar edges to the counter and returns the bishop's handshake, hearty and invasive.

"Wreaking havoc downtown," says Einar as he sits. "I'll have a Sprite." This to the waitress who has materialized with a coffee pot. She smiles, retreating with the pot and leaving the fragrance that Einar always holds in his head like a warm chestnut. It is the rich, distinctive smell he first experienced when he spent a childhood summer helping out on his uncle's ranch in Idaho.

"We're gonna need sandbag crews," says the bishop. He jabs at the front page of the newspaper. "No one's ever seen anything like this. Entire town of Thistle under fifty feet of water. Railroad can't get through Spanish Fork Canyon down to the coal mines in Price. Makes you wonder if the second coming of the Lord isn't upon us."

"There's M.A.s floating down the gutters on North Temple," says Einar. "I guess that's gotta mean something."

"No kidding?" says the bishop. "Wonder if the prophet knows about it."

"I would've stopped to help 'em out," says Einar referring to the ministering angels. "You know, get some of 'em at least cross the street—but the traffic was ridin' my . . . pushin' me from behind." Einar looks over the bishop's shoulder when he says this, hoping his half-lie will float past the bishop and into the corner of the diner where a broom stands.

"Haven't talked with you for a while, Brother Allred. How's your father and the pipeline business?" Einar understands they are talking in code. To talk to the bishop means to confess something. Einar considers what he might confess to his bishop over Sprite and the newspaper at Ruth's Diner. Aside from drinking the dreaded bean beverage, and the stray erection he lingers over in the shower, there is the little item of the temple where not only the Great Work for the dead is performed but marriages for the living—as in his sister-in-law's coming up next week. Yesterday, he told Donna he will not be going to the wedding.

"Why not?" she said, a spoon of yellow puree suspended in front of their son's drooly-lipped mouth above the tray of the high chair. The boy looked at him and smiled, his mouth full of the stuff, and Einar felt a stab of affection for the little guy, a reminder that no matter what catastrophe might befall him and Donna and the whole world for that matter, it was enough that he had had this one moment to love this sticky child. Even so, as he looked over his shoulder to check on the boy's twin sister, he steeled himself before answering his wife's question.

"Recommend's expired," he said. How could he tell her that he had no plans to renew it? He turned abruptly toward the kitchen where he waited for the squall to come from behind, the sudden cloudburst that was Donna's trademark. When they were dating he admired her outspoken nature, so different from the other young women's. Yet, ever since the twins were born, she and the sisterhood at the women's auxiliary seemed to have crocheted their faith into a noose that Donna brandished whenever she sensed Einar wasn't living up to the standard. Which lately seemed to be often.

"S. Einar Hinckley Packer Leavitt Allred," she said, and he knew he was in deep trouble. She poked him in the chest with the half-filled spoon. "Bishop Mitchell is on to you, and it's making us all look bad. Would you like me to make an appointment for an interview, or will you be doing it? I'm waiting." The puree dripped down his fresh T-shirt.

That was the squall yesterday, which actually aroused Einar, as these squalls are wont to do. But what Donna does not know is that Einar's "recommend," the result of an annual worthiness interview with the bishop, has not simply expired. It *cannot* be renewed. To make ends meet for the past six months, Einar has been secretly spending their tithing, the requisite contribution necessary to pass through the temple's Checkpoint Charlie and gain access to the wedding of Donna's sister.

Einar looks at Bishop Mitchell. This meeting could not be a coincidence. He has never seen the bishop at Ruth's Diner, known not only for its insufferably crabby owner, but for its coffee-drinking "gentile" clientele. That was why Einar went so far up Emigration Canyon in the morning for his coffee. The only Mormons at Ruth's were like his aunt and uncle in Idaho, coffee and liquor-imbibing Jack Mormons who cannot get into the temple anymore for family weddings. The kind of Mormon Einar is fast becoming.

"I have a confession to make, bishop," says Einar.

Back in the city, the Sunday School Burglar parks along the gentle grade of 2nd East Street and turns off the engine. He pulls his baseball cap down to better shade his eyes. The gutters are brimming with a soup, rushing with purpose yet somehow silent in the concrete troughs. Outside the car, the air is preternaturally heavy. A flock of birds skitters out of a tree, dips sharply toward the ground then makes formation and bolts west. Nothing else seems to be in motion, as if the earth were holding its breath, waiting.

For two years, while serving what has, since the uptight M.A.s' arrival, become a required church proselytizing "mission," Rex was known simply as "Elder Jorgensen." And even though he resented being shipped off at age nineteen to Denmark for two years to preach the Mormon gospel in his family's ancestral home, he actually came to like his new moniker. Not because it was an ecclesiastical title, but because he was no longer called "Rex." But now, back at home, he is faced again with the one thing he hates most about himself. His name. The first initial, "Y," doesn't stand for anything, which sometimes gets him into trouble when he is filling out tax forms. And he can't just call himself "Y." ("The name's Y." "Why?" "Yes." "Excuse me?" "I don't know why." "What?" "No . . . Y.") Much too confusing.

So he goes by "Rex," one of those antique names stemming from the days of polygamy when families had, literally, scores of children and unused names were scarce. To him, "Rex" is unbearable, the name of a backroom school janitor who always smells funny, or a drifter waiting in line at the shelter near the Greyhound station. Not to mention the petulant TV-ad cat with the same name. Rex takes some solace from the new name with which he was first endowed in the temple as a departing missionary—a name he can be proud of. "John," meaning "Yahweh is gracious." And more importantly to Rex, the name recalls John McEnroe, the fiery, bad-ass tennis player who destroys his racket after losing a game and verbally abuses the chair umpires. The problem is, the new name is not for this life, but for the next and, per protocol, it can never be spoken to anyone—not even to one's own future wife. More evidence that the universe has it out for him.

It was nine months ago when Rex was struck by a plan. It happened while he stood during sacrament meeting so the congregation could "sustain" him as the new assistant scoutmaster, and it was then, with old Sister Vogel's face beaming up at him like a searchlight, that it occurred to him that everyone who lived within four square blocks was at that moment sitting in the chapel, every house within the ward boundary vibrating only to the sound of a roof-installed evaporative cooler. Empty. Waiting to be burgled. "All in favor of sustaining Brother Rex," he remembers his own bishop intoning at the podium, "indicate so by raising the right hand." My sorry, mismatched name justifies any career choice, thought Rex as he sat back down on the pew in church. Why wait for the next life to be justified and recompensed? In short, Rex the blue-blood had a revelation, as bluebloods are wont to have. It was unorthodox, but what true revelation isn't? (Maybe he *was* a believer after all.)

Of course Rex wasn't going to case his own neighborhood. He would plant himself in the foothills of the wealthier snob hill domiciles and wait. That was twelve casings, followed by eleven hits ago. The Sunday School Burglar has even made the papers.

On the sidewalk, coming toward Rex, are two dogs, collared, but free-ranging, a black lab and what looks like a cross between a shepherd and a malamute. They zig-zag on the sidewalk, as if on a string operated from above. They sniff at the rushing water, whimper and turn, circling back around where they were earlier, then starting in a new direction. It occurs to Rex that these dogs do not know each other, and that any moment they could turn on one another, not out of some kind of alpha-dog angling, but out of inexplicable fright. In the gutter Rex notices a stray name that must have been caught by the wind or a passing car barreling up the hill and deposited here in a temporary eddy before it breaks out and continues its journey back downhill. The name is Rex Jarlsberg, the recently deceased bantam weight boxer whose real name was Reginald. Not like Rex, who is just a "Rex."

Tomorrow, the Sunday School Burglar promises himself, he will take a few weeks off from his new career, maybe get out of town, lay low. "Place is starting to give me the creeps," he mutters to himself.

Back at Ruth's Diner: "I have a confession to make, bishop," says Einar. Bishop Mitchell carefully folds the newspaper and lays it on the counter. A mantle of ecclesiastical solemnity descends on him. He laces his fingers together on the counter and leans in. But before Einar can say anything the diner begins to shake, and the roar of the creek out back crackles and booms. It sounds as if a train were barreling toward the tiny canyon diner. The broom dances out of the corner in three small bristled hops before falling to the floor with a smack, and old Ruth herself makes a rare appearance in her flowered house dress, a forgotten cigarette clinging to her trembling lips.

The bishop's face goes white.

By the time Einar and the bishop get to Einar's truck, the narrow road is filled with mud six inches thick, and the smell of clay and rock and uprooted trees is everywhere. Ruth, clinging to her broom, has refused to evacuate with them, so it is just Einar, Bishop Mitchell and the waitress, whose white uniform pants are now muddy up to her crotch so that it looks as if she is wearing hot pants. Down the canyon fly the three of them in Einar's truck, dodging the biggest of the rocks and sliding haphazardly over sludge that shoots over the front of the hood and onto the windshield while underneath it cakes up in the wheel wells and grinds noisily.

"Better get to that sandbagging," says Einar to the bishop. In between them sits the waitress, trying to avoid straddling the stick shift with her red legs.

"Will Ruth be alright?" she asks, a hand flat against the ceiling of the cab as they fling themselves down the canyon like a giant bat at dusk.

❧

The following day is the Sabbath, and mid-way through priesthood meeting word is received from the pulpit in every ward along the Wasatch Front that, Sunday or not, the ox is in the mire—up to its prepuce in runoff. All able-bodied persons are needed immediately for sandbagging. Over at the cathedral, the Very Reverend Juan Sanchez gets a whispered message at the altar from an acolyte, flaps through the 10 a.m. mass double-time and shoos everyone out onto the street. All seven of the valley's major drainages are well above flood levels. The city at the foot of the hemorrhaging mountains is under siege, every one of its arteries swollen and purging. The canyons are rumbling, crying in the wilderness. And in the city, sandbagged rivers quickly begin to take form, directing red, muddy water down State Street, Thirteenth East and Ninth East Streets toward the Jordan River and an expanding Great Salt Lake.

The Great Work of name extraction and saving the dead slip-slides to an oozing halt. The temple doors closed, its workers sent home. M.A.s are swept away by the thousands along with the names they have mined from the public record. Some of the tiny workers are rumored to be hiding out on the second floor of the Hotel Utah where there is angry talk of organizing. And ensconced in the quiet, upper rooms of the temple itself, the white-haired prophet peers out of one of the distinctive, oval-shaped windows faceted into the thick granite walls. A modern-day Noah in his ark. For a long time he watches his charges, still in their Sunday best, high-stepping through ankle-deep water and carting sandbags. Occasionally, one of the workers bends over and hooks the tail of a "g" or the crossbar of a "t" of one of the many names being swept away.

Above, the sky is as dark blue as the blood of the freshly resurrected dead. Blue as the blood of God the Father and his Son Jesus. And all this red water, pouring out of the hills like the blood of a true mortal . . . well, it is disconcerting to the weary prophet who is the mortal closest to becoming a full-blown blueblood even before he dies and goes to the celestial kingdom. "I'm not sure I can handle any of this," he says, and the heavy drapes on the oval window fall back as he shuffles away in his white slippers.

Even Father Sanchez, a Catholic, is aware of the local belief that what makes one immortal is that one's blood becomes slowly replaced with a spiritual fluid, matter so fine as to elude the scientific lens. It is a fluid void of the corrosive effects of blood. It is "blood" that has been blued by faith and obedience and is therefore no longer the carrier of death. What's known as blueblood is the very font of one's exaltation —not like the M.A.s, the ministering class—but exaltation as the gods are exalted. It is the bluebloods—the improbably righteous—who will eventually stake their claim in the heavens as new gods, as the creators of new worlds and of new souls.

In this valley, Father Sanchez has often had to explain to visiting priests, "one aspires to blood that is blue, to resurrection as a deity and to be with one's exalted loved ones for eternity. This is the reason for name extraction." Yes, even the good father knows that saving ordinances must be performed in the temple for every person who has ever lived and died. So that all of humankind can merit their way into blueblood for the eternities. When Father Sanchez first arrived at the diocese, he wrote a stinging newspaper editorial about the practice of "saving the dead" by proxy baptism. But now? He grudgingly accepts it. One year after his death, per stipulation, his own name will show up in the temple, and he will be baptized vicariously, and by the true priesthood, so that in the hereafter his blood will be . . . blued.

In the meantime, he maintains his Roman faith as much as he can among these peculiar people.

❧

Despite this understanding of a blood substitute spawned by obedience to a higher law, Einar—father of twins and husband to a full-of-faith and anxious wife—does not stop his foraging for morning coffee, an intractable entitlement that colors Einar's blood pink if not red. On *this* Sunday morning, when he gets a call from the ward house that they need his truck up Little Cottonwood Canyon to carry sand baggers, he uses it as the day's excuse to get his morning fix. To stave off criticism or invasive questioning by his fellow ward members, he puts on his Sunday uniform—white shirt and tie—before heading out to throw bags on the Lord's Day. On the way out, he meets a teary-eyed Donna at the door.

"What is it, muffin breath?" he says, and she bursts into tears. The perpetual platelets of anxiety that course through her veins bubble up to her eyes and flood forth at his question —casual (and fearful) as it is.

"I . . . (sob) . . . want . . . (inhale) . . . to be . . ." she begins waving her hand in front of her contorted face, struggling to collect herself. "I want you at my sister's wedding, Einar. Everyone will notice that you're not there. They'll wonder why, and they'll wonder the worst." Einar wishes he had taken that load of M.A.s to dry ground the day before. His report back to Donna of the deed would have stanched this moment, he thinks, standing with his hand on the knob to the front door. But now, she is sobbing in front of him so loudly that the twins begin crying as well. Jenny sits down hard on her diaper, her lower lip curling in under fat cheeks, and her brother Jason begins a wind-up like his toy choo-choo train before letting out a piercing whistle shriek.

Einar reaches for Donna, wrapping his arms around her and patting at her moist back. "Now, now . . ." he says, galvanizing into the family patriarch. "Look at you, all of you. What is all this? We already have enough water works out there without . . ." He kisses Donna on the forehead and cheeks, and then she reaches for Jason. Einar instinctively starts for Jenny. They stand, jostling the twins.

Isn't that enough? he thinks to himself later after leaving home and driving along Wasatch Boulevard to the mouth of Little Cottonwood Canyon, sans his morning coffee. It isn't the promises of the hereafter that make him want to love his wife. It is her body, the sweet sag of her postpartum can, the fragrant notch in her neck. Her smell. The twins are just a happy, natural consequence of that. It isn't because of her righteousness that he wants her—although Einar is the first to acknowledge that Donna's demonstrated rectitude initially helped close the deal with his family. No. It is the way Donna's breasts move under that limp blouse when she bounces up and down during volleyball. The pounding of blood in his head and in his loins. It is that, and it is more. It is the tang of dirt and pine in the morning before he fires up his backhoe for a day's work on the canyon roads. The distant sparkle of the lake as he drives, sweaty and weary, back home for dinner. It is the way the sun bakes his back when he is washing the truck. The comforting click of Donna's Sunday heels on the kitchen floor as they head out to church. The way his daughter sleeps on her stomach, her knees up under her belly like a Muslim at prayer. Isn't all that why they were here?

Why all this posturing toward eternity? The cool, antiseptic embalming of immortality? The Great Work of temple ordinances, genealogy—saving the dead? What doth it all profit? The most excitement he has ever had on any Sunday is today, with people's homes roiling in danger, the regularity of church meetings torn to shreds as everyone drops their scriptures for a shovel.

❧

Meanwhile Rex is delirious. Not only has everyone in the neighborhood gone to church but evacuated wholesale in a sort of reverse rapture down to the valley where they are now filling sandbags, assembling baffle boards and lustily singing,

Put your shoulder to the wheel, push a-long.
Do your duty with a heart full of song.
We all have work, let no one shirk,
Put your shoulder to the wheel. . . .

They pass sand bags hand-to-hand, exhilarated by the warm silt in their shoes, the splash of the mountain blood in their faces. The young mothers, taking snapshots and fixing sandwiches, move with their children to higher and higher ground. Even the prophet, having swapped out his slippers for boots, has gone against the counsel of his more circumspect apostles, and shown up with a smile and a wave at the exhilarated crowd.

The streets above the city are so empty that Rex thinks he must be cheating the universe. He whistles as he closes his car trunk on the spoils of the first two hits. Every resentment harbored deep in his sternum seems now to be uncoiling like a spring. When he gets to the third and final house, he walks up the arc-ed driveway and straight through the front door triumphantly singing, "The morning breaks, the shadows flee..."

❧

At the mouth of Little Cottonwood Canyon, Einar loads his truck with two other men and sandbags. Then they head up. Their destination is the Granite Mountain Records Vault, embedded deep in the north wall of the canyon. The very headwaters of the Great Work.

Today the protective vaults are threatened by the rock in which they rest, once thought to be immovable by quake or flood. Einar has been here as a teenager when his class toured the stacks of microfiche to which librarians were transferring the records. Brother Schmidt, a bald man with a pointed nose, was dwarfed by the shelves, and when he spoke of how much of the vast project of collecting the names of all earthly inhabitants had actually been completed, he compared it to five inches of the one hundred-yard football field at the U's Rice Stadium. The students, including Einar, all gasped at the enormity of the task that lay ahead for the salvation of humanity, and Brother Schmidt smiled.

But now the massive name extraction program is imperiled. When Einar and the sandbaggers make the hairpin turn into the parking lot of the giant vaults, they are horrified to see water and mud spurting out from under the six heavy Mosler doors, and old Brother Schmidt, trembling and crying, his hands placed forcefully on the surface of the middle door, up to his ankles in rushing water and mud.

"*Gå opp!*" shouts Einar in what little Norwegian he's picked up from his maternal grandmother. "Pony up, brethren!" And he shifts into four-wheel drive. "Levee the bags, beginning over there, berms over there." He points to crumbling rock on the east wall. The plan is to keep the flow moving out and away from the doors, through the parking lot and down the canyon, so that the doors can be safely opened and the back-up in the catacomb of names minimized.

Above the working men is another vault—the cloudless sky which lies impenetrable to the drama of shoring up the mountain, and suddenly Einar senses the futility of it all. He has lived the measured life some twenty odd years—living by covenant, by program, by sheer dint of self-control. But all of it, as in this mountain cracking as it is now below the towering peaks, suddenly seems both inevitable and awesome. It is a world that eludes a prophet's prophecy, a world that is necessary and catastrophic and limns Einar's brain, his heart and his balls all at the same time. Something he has glimpsed in determined movements of his children as they push back against the world while simultaneously surrendering to it, a kind of tango that innervates the creation rather than depletes, cools and sterilizes creation, arouses it.

It is color as opposed to structure. It is how blood returns indelibly to the color red.

❧

Once inside the third house, Rex feels empty instead of energized. This is different. He tries to organize his thoughts, make a plan, a sweep through the house that has the lived-in baby smell of twin toddlers, something stale, something sour. He looks at the pictures on the wall, of a man and a woman in wedding attire, the tuxedo-ed man stiff and broad as a nutcracker, she, in practiced repose—lace everywhere. He no longer believes in the eternities, or marriage, and now in his element he should feel the relief of acting as he truly is, at shedding his usual performance of the righteous, recently-returned missionary, the assistant scoutmaster looking for a wife. But he feels more unease than relief.

He sits back on the couch and remembers the last time he has been this smart. Or at least thought so at the time. It was when he was in Copenhagen. He was training a new missionary companion, one Elder Stewart, nineteen-years-old and fresh off the plane from Utah. The two of them have just been told by their number one prospective convert that she has decided not to go through with her baptism the next day.

"Can I ask you a question?" says Elder Stewart that night as they readied for bed, their gloom punctuated by a persistent Danish drizzle. "Do you sometimes question what we're doing out here? That it's really all that we say it is?" It is a moment for Rex that seems trite in the face of his own doubts that have long turned secretly cankerous, and he takes enormous pleasure in telling the young man, "You don't really think any of us actually believe any of this, do you?" And then, with all the malice he can muster, "Oh . . . sorry . . . do you?" The next day Rex awakens to an empty apartment. Elder Stewart has left. Gone home.

Tyrannosaurus Rex. Just living up to a name he never chose.

When the mudslide starts to splinter the front door, Rex first thinks it is a pack of mad dogs. For a moment, he actually considers looking through the door's peephole, but then he finds himself instinctively backing up toward the stairs that lead to the first floor and, hopefully, a way out. But downstairs he finds a river of the red silt that is becoming thicker by the moment, piling up against the sliding glass door like gravel in the bottom of an aquarium. The door leads to the back yard and down the steep slope of the mountain. He hears the sound of something knocking—three hard mallet knocks—and turns to watch the mud pour out of the heating vents in the living room where he stands, shell-shocked.

Rex is encased in mud, dead, and thus finally answering to the name, "John," his secret new name given to him in the temple. Outside, the chimney spouts mud. Red, coarse and hot.

❧

The western-most vault gives way first, the men barely able to snag Brother Schmidt and scramble up a rise to safety. The great door, rounded at the top, begins to sigh and pop. Bolts with heads the size of silver dollars wriggle loose and then, consecutively, from the bottom of the door up, shoot out of their respective bays like missiles. Granite rock splits all around the door which after the slightest, quietest of moments crumples like tin, and there is a rush of water, red mud and stone. The men scramble further up the rise, barely able to shout at each other over the chaos of the mountain giving way. Then a second vault collapses, and out of the cracking granite caves come the names, first two of them stumbling up and out of the rubble, newborn foals of Anson F. Livingstone and Abu Jabbar—followed by a rush of others—Susan Channing Jones, Markus Randall Klink, Solange LaCoeur, John Jasper Jenkins, and then a whole stampede of Mohammed Alis. All of them materialize from the microfiche and film records of marriage indices, parish lists, census reports, pilgrim registers, necrologies, all of the names pouring out, bumping up against the embankments, swirling around a single sandbag still poking its ears above the deluge. The names move out and around the corner of the parking lot, where two of them—Artaxiad and Ibrahim—simultaneously rise out of the water like jumping fish, shiny in the afternoon light, then down, down toward the mouth of the canyon.

The shifting, water-logged mountains continue to open their veins with a groan. Mountain blood mixes with the fecund undergrowth of juniper pine that clings to granite flanks by mere tendrils, it turns over and flees downhill, west toward the valleys and the lake. Under the blinding, high-desert sun, the threat to home and body is also the carrier of life. It sops the desert floor, it pushes back against the temple doors, it laps tantalizingly around the giant tower of the corporate church. It seeps through, bowls-over and undermines the holy city with its natural, alkaline charms. And out of Little Cottonwood Canyon the wild, earthen blood carries millions of names—Lawrence McAllister, J.B. Hunan, Chaim Lieberman, Cynthia Moy, Marilyn Virzi, David Kerekang, someone Said. The names spin blithely downstream, bruised but happy. Stories will surface later about a Ninth South Street eddy where a family of Tiengs from Cambodia was caught with a family of Lees from Korea, and about how a Jacob Fleischer was hooked into the "O" of an Omar Nader. Red Butte river and City Creek tangling with Parley's and the Cottonwood Canyons waterways. The pond in Liberty Park will, for a time, be known as Alphabet Soup.

From the mountain where Einar has climbed above the vault to wait out the flood, he looks out over the valley and watches the silver names tripping over boulders and around buildings—and of course each other as they head out to the Jordan River and the mighty, bloated great and salted lake. There they lie flat against the still surface of the brackish water, the late-in-the-day sun reflecting off them like light off the iridescent scales of cutthroat trout. Einar's skin is ruddy with the pulse of life flowing beneath it, the veins in his arms blue through skin, but red as mountain mud. With their work in ruins, thinks Einar, maybe the M.A.s will pack up and head out. Standing there and looking over the valley, the curious sense of relief he's felt since the vault has given way now turns to compassion for them, for the M.A.s, burdened with names, and he wonders if maybe he should suggest to the bishop, when they all get back to the ward, that they start some kind of retraining program for M.A.s. A Perpetual Emigration Fund for Ministering Angels.

Then overhead Einar hears a sound, like a bird. When he looks up he sees Ruth from the diner, last seen hunched over her broom. Now she is balanced on that broom, gliding on a warm updraft while she tries to light a cigarette. He thinks about his Donna and the twins, safe at his in-laws on the valley's west side. Then S. Einar Hinckley Packer Leavitt Allred finds himself craving a cup of aromatic coffee, black.

Dreamcatcher

Outside the book depository, the night watchman listens intently for the great horned owl that frequents the neighborhood. He finishes his cigarette, lights a second, and moves across the loading dock, chancing being seen. At dusk the crime lights—one tacked to the front of the narrow, three-story brick building, the other hanging over the back fire escape—blinker on to an industrial hum. And at precisely eight o'clock the sprinklers, calibrated to reach the corners of the manicured lawn and no farther, spring to life, all designed, it seems to him, to keep the out-of-place 1912 building under the radar. Inconspicuous.

Adjacent to the building, behind the eight-foot iron fence with spikes atop, the parking lot is segmented by lines, cracks in the surface filled by a contractor who comes in every year with a tar wand. Though the gates are flung open Sunday mornings to allow parking for congregants of two small protestant churches across the alley, the doors of the old Hyland Telephone & Telegraph Exchange remain locked to the public. The watchman, whose name is Rell, cocks his head to the left. Still no sound or sight of the bird.

The owl flies over Cummings chocolate shop, over the high tension wires of 8th South, over the First Ward house. It climbs high on a sudden updraft and circles back over Trolley Square, then sinks toward 4th South's fast food row. It is Tuesday night, the light rail clangs down the hill from the university. Somewhere over the Cathedral of the Madeleine, it goes into a stoop and retrieves the first dream of the night, a tiny black-and-white narrative of curious workmanship, the dream of a homeless man asleep on the rectory lawn, an empty bottle let loose at his side.

In The Avenues the raptor circles an art deco apartment building where it glimpses a sleeping man curled into the side of his partner who sits reading in bed, his eyes intent on the page. The sleeping man's embodied dream rises into the air, angry to have been pulled from its mother's teat. It burns in the bird's talons like a flaming aleph, then weeps bitterly and resignedly as it hangs pinched high above the streets. Tonight, for the winged dreamcatcher, there will be sighing dreams, restless dreams of ambition and hubris and the purple-tinged dreams of victory. On the west side near the tortilla factory the dreams will carry the odor of Aztec battles borne over the ancient fields of Meso-America, and as the owl drifts over Glendale, they will sound like ocean waves and look like a Tongan moon. The dreams writhe in its talons for only seconds before settling in, taking in the view of the lights, the cold symmetry of the streets, the terrifying beauty of the mountains.

The owl perches in a tree near a house, attracted by the hold of intimate conversation, the night's dreams still held fast and quiet under talon. A woman is sitting on the back porch, the lights off. A man stands next to her, a foot planted on the first step leading up to the door, arms folded across his chest. The man wants his revenge and the woman wants hers. Their separate but equal needs rise up and hover in front of the bird who looks at them as only an owl can look at dreams of desire —dispassionately. Then, in a single action, it plucks them out of the air while bolting from the tree at the sound of the screen door slamming. On the way out it dips over Research Park. There, it snags a small, undefined dream of future peer-reviewed honor from a woman in a white lab coat, her head resting on a desk, the fluorescent light unrelentingly bright.

At the place in the city known as Gilgal the owl perches atop a giant, multi-segmented bird house. Below lie myriad flat stones with scriptures and hymns inscribed on their surfaces. Stranger still are the sculptures in the shadows of the surrounding trees. There is a sphinx and in her face is found the countenance of the founding Mormon prophet, Joseph Smith—broad forehead, prominent cheekbones above a receding chin. The eyes are bulging and sad. The owl perches on one of the boulders hauled down from Little Cottonwood Canyon decades earlier by Bishop Childs, the sculptor of this weird place. The bird waits for the sphinx to speak, but the sphinx only stares toward the garden entrance, her haunches and front paws anchored in un-hewn stone.

Finally, the sphinx blinks. "There isn't anything to say," says the sphinx.

"You say that every night," returns the owl. "But then you always say something." The sphinx is silent. Then, "It's been warm enough now that I can feel my paws, all four of them." The owl shifts its weight, hoping it will encourage more than pleasantries from the sphinx. A pungent whiff from the bread factory next door momentarily makes the owl swoon, and it nearly releases the bundled dreams.

"It wasn't what he thought it would be," says the sphinx, nodding in the direction of the bishop-sculptor who, like her, is memorialized in stone. What he called his "iron pen" is now cemented at his side, the tip broken off by vandals. The bishop's eyes are vacant above jowls. "He's disappointed," the sphinx continues. "He wanted to create for believers a sanctuary from perilous times by transferring the truth to them."

"And did it work? Are the believers safe now?"

"No. Truth does not translate from one tongue to another, let alone simply transfer, as a transaction. After all, I am *still* silent." They both look at the bishop.

"Maybe your silence will keep their minds alert," says the owl. "They need to know there are things they cannot know. You don't find buried treasure as it exists here—truth written in stone."

"No. People must create their own gardens. This is why the bishop is disappointed. Wasted effort it seems."

The owl is still, long enough for the whistle of a distant train to fade. It is getting late.

"Tomorrow," says the owl. And it flies away.

It rests on the roof of the book depository, above Rell. Then it lifts off, flies out and back around, this time perching on the inner rim of the chimney. It teeters as the wind picks up. It gives its melancholy call to the night. It surveys the scene—Smith's Food & Drug lined with poplars, the foothills rising to the bench where the fault line runs below the massifs of the Wasatch Range. To the south lies the ever-expanding city. The owl's head pivots northward, a breeze riffling the pin feathers of its breast. It blinks toward the city center.

The owl loses its balance. In that instant there is a sucking sound.

Rell hears the owl calling, but this time it sounds as if the bird is falling away. Do owls enter that state of mind known as *yarak*, he wonders. Like other raptors? To him an owl always seems more brooding than fierce, less a hunter than simply a silencer of the hunted. He is on his third cigarette. He is a man thick in the neck and chest, forty years old with fine, blonde hair, a sparse beard, a man who for survival must define himself by a single category—a drunk. That's what Rell's six months of sobriety have taught him. ("It doesn't matter why I drink, only that I stop.")

It will be another three months before Rell can get his driver's license back so that he can return to birding. In the meantime he visits the aviary at nearby Liberty Park and watches the raptors, which perch singly and flightless. Afterwards, he retires to the gift shop where, earlier this week the volunteer intern located a book for him. "When do they let the hawks and the owls fly?" asked Rell of the intern, a native from the Pima Tribe.

"When they escape," said the young man sincerely.

Back on the loading dock, Rell stubs the end of the cigarette into the sole of his shoe, and then pockets the butt. He wonders where the owl might have gone. Listens for it. The sounds of the city seem to align themselves with the stillness of his mood.

"You could lose your job for that," says a voice to his left. Startled, Rell moves back against the brick. A man materializes out of the dark. He is smaller than Rell, somewhat older, with a white shirt, tie and a light windbreaker. He climbs the cement stairs of the dock, white knuckles grasping the railing. How did *he* get in through the fence, Rell wonders. Then he hears the jangling of keys.

"No one told me to expect anyone," says Rell.

"Do you obey the Word of Wisdom only when you're being watched? I could report this to the work program which has rules."

"It won't happen again," says Rell, and he finds himself slipping into a familiar shame, one he knew well as early as junior high and epitomized by the response of his schoolmates to his odd name—"Smelly Rell Fell To Hell." It was the same shame he later tried to drown by drinking first beer and then the harder stuff. He remembers how his father had picked him up at the airport when Rell returned early from the two-year mission he was expected to complete, never asking his son why he was bringing dishonor to the family name. Then, before the subject of his unexpected return could come up the next day, his disgrace was eclipsed by the murders of two citizens followed the next day by the severe injury of a third . . . by pipe bombs. Through the next months, as details of these horrors came to light, Rell supposed he had only been saved from having to explain himself to his father and everyone else in the ward by nothing less than the explosions in the city of saints.

That was twenty years ago.

"The first step in repentance is to confess," continues the man in the windbreaker who makes an institutional attempt at warmth by smiling. Rell returns the favor. He doesn't need to confess his smoking to anyone. He just needs to stop.

"I came to check the stores for a misplaced delivery," says the man, lifting his chin, a veritable pointer. "In the basement."

"They briefed me on the basement."

"What did they tell you?" says the man a little too fast.

"Just that there was no need for me to go down there. I don't even have a key."

"No. You don't have a key to the basement," says the man. He uses his full weight to open the heavy door to the building. "*I* have the keys to the basement."

"Less for me to worry about, right?" says Rell as he follows him in. He craves another cigarette. They walk past the desk, a banker's lamp pooling light on unread newspapers and Rell's book, *Flight Identification of Rocky Mountain Raptors*. The man unlocks the door to the chain link cage that separates the entry from the stores. He walks toward the back wall of the building where stairs lead to the basement. Halfway there, he turns. "You can stay there, please. I'll only be a minute."

They stare at each other, over the man's chin, the bell light above them swaying, shadows sparring with boxes of church manuals, handbooks and maps. Rell silently reminds himself that in this, his new life of sobriety, everything is real, everything is raw. He steps forward. "What are you hiding down there, anyway?" he asks. "Rumor has it the Church has a lot to hide," says Rell. "Especially since the bombings, you know."

It had been a few years now, bombs planted by a religious document forger trying to cover his tracks. Rell only remembers snippets of the convoluted story. He simply remembers that they caught the forger, an embittered man accidentally injured by his own bomb—the third to go off—and that there had been a plea bargain. More cogent for Rell is the memory of his father who stayed fixed to the television and forgot about his son, home early from his mission.

"Actually, I don't know," says the man while giving Rell a knowing smile. "Are you accusing the Church of lying?"

Rell feigned disinterest. By now he knew well how to feign. He remembers thinking that perhaps he should have been one of the bomber's victims. As a young man, Rell had become obsessed with the relics of his faith, just as these victims had, willing for at least a time to deal with a kind of devil to prove the church's fantastical truth claims, of angels without wings, golden plates etched with "reformed Egyptian," a sword once owned by a powerful man named Laban who lived in biblical times.

What Rell's father did not know was that his son had failed as a missionary because he had succumbed to pursuit of material proof of Truth, with a capital "T." Rell coveted the perpetually missing icons of his faith's foundational stories. And when his pursuit failed to yield the proofs—the relics of the stories he was supposed to testify to as a missionary—he began to drink in earnest.

The man stands squarely in front of Rell, and then, in a single breath says, "What am I hiding down there? That's a very good question, Brother Jensen. But Heavenly Father only adds knowledge line-upon-line to those who *first* keep his commandments." It occurs to Rell that he hasn't done any kind of close inventory of the depository. He peers about now, as if searching for something. The man continues. "When I feel resentful, Rell, I find it helpful if someone reminds me that in this world we live by faith, not by sight, and that sometimes the answers we are given by those in authority are the *only* ones we are ready to hear. Isn't that what Alcoholics Anonymous asks *you* to do?"

"Sounds too much like being asked to follow in blind obedience," says Rell. "And no, that's not what recovery is about, if you must know." He is annoyed that the stranger knows his full name and that he knows about his meetings. (So much for the anonymous part.)

There is the sound of the owl, again, curiously faded and fallen away, and the man instinctively looks toward the arched window—bricked in—then tilts his head to locate the sound. He's probably right, thinks Rell. I don't need to know what's downstairs. Then Rell has an inspiration. He turns to leave the cage, to go back to his desk.

"The basement," says the man, stepping forward. "You must never go into the basement."

"Maybe *you* should never go into the basement," says Rell who does not turn around, but continues to the desk and the small circle of light. His retort surprises even him. He feigns disinterest in the conversation, picking up a newspaper, turning a page. He waits for the man who Rell now knows *has* to speak. He seems to Rell to have no choice in the matter, that he is an addict in his own way. At length, he looks back into the cage. The man stands with his hands stuffed in the pockets of his windbreaker.

"There are things you don't know."

"Don't doubt that," says Rell.

"It's not like the Vatican which has had two thousand years to build a convincing explanation around the remaining evidence. Our church is less than one-hundred-and-seventy-five-years old. There's still a lot of material to process." Rell doesn't know exactly what the man is referring to. "The truth needs a space," the man insists, his voice rising, "a space free of any distractions to develop as it should. To emerge as it was destined to." He pauses, turns almost in a three-sixty, looks up at the ceiling. Rell can feel a power shift in the room. He fishes for a cigarette, lights it in front of his visitor, draws in the smoke so far that he doesn't know where it could possibly be going. The man waits for him to exhale. He watches the smoke curl up toward the ceiling and spread out, disappearing in the darkness above.

"One day I was working at Welfare Square, giving tours to New Yorkers and Germans," the man reports, "and I was told I had a new job." He squints at the residual smoke, his lips curled. "When I asked about the door to the basement, they told me there was only the boiler down there. That the door needed to be kept locked. Except for maintenance." He looks at Rell, then continues. "They assumed that I wouldn't wonder. That I was some kind of grunt. This was just after the bombings," he continued. "The FBI was everywhere." Again, a pause. He has told this story before in his head, to himself. Never to another person. "Later, up at the Church offices, they made a big scene of throwing open the door to the vault of the

First Presidency. 'See?' They said to the agents. 'Nothing. Nothing but old deeds.'"

"Who is they? You keep saying 'they'."

"The FBI."

"No. You keep saying *they* threw open the vault. *They* . . ."

"The Brethren, of course!"

"Of course," says Rell. "So why are you telling me?" And he takes another pull off his cigarette, then turns away.

"What I'm trying to say is that The Brethren moved the contents of the vault here!" The man is breathing hard now, his face flushed. It occurs to Rell that he isn't the only one who doesn't know why this man, somehow looking chilled in the summer heat, is here.

"They moved all the old deeds?" asks Rell, angling for more information. "If that's all there was, then why. . . ." The man turns in frustration. He walks to the top of the stairwell and flips a switch. A light throws itself up the steps and into the man's face of angles. He seems older to Rell in the yellow light and even more anxious with the stairwell before him.

"My job is to hide the relics!" says the man, turning to face Rell. "The relics no one knows exist. The relics which would destroy the people's faith if they knew, if they examined them and compared them to how the truth otherwise must emerge. How it *has* emerged." Suddenly, the man turns back toward the stairwell, startled by a sound. His face contorts. Rell puts out his unfinished cigarette, this time on the floor. He moves into the cage.

"What is that?" Rell goes to the top of the stairwell. The man creeps down, a hand pressed against the concrete wall as if to hold himself up. A light bulb, pinned to the wall below and behind its own private cage, burns furiously. At the bottom of the stair stands a door of brushed steel to which the man, now trembling, has pressed an ear. The man looks back up at Rell. The man puts a finger to his lips and shows Rell a set of gold keys, then gives Rell a single nod. He unlocks first the silver padlock and then the dead bolt. He stops. A muffled clambering starts from inside the room. The man turns, eyes ablaze. "You're the night watchman. You go in," he says.

Inside the room, Rell stumbles. While he fishes for a match, the man turns a switch and light suddenly fills the room. It seems for a moment to flutter and buzz, like an insect all around their heads, then grows in strength until it is as bright as noon day. Rell spins half around in the glory of it. For it seems to him that he has entered a space much larger than the building can contain. He becomes the electrical charge looking for a place to ground, and then the sensation stops. In the hollow of his mind he realizes that his need to know is his real addiction, not drinking, just like the man who has entered the room and turned on the light. Rell recognizes it as their joint disease, and it is delicious.

The room slowly becomes drawn before Rell, shelves, floor-to-ceiling along the walls stashed with metal boxes and an occasional wooden trunk with hardware that bespeaks a different era. There are plastic tags, attached with wire to the containers and which recount the contents—"Brigham's Peep Stone," "The 'Lost' Manuscript (116 pages)." There is everything in the room, from amulets to Masonic aprons and from divining rods to mummified salamanders.

The man has moved from the door and is trailing Rell as he advances down the length of the shelves, reads the tags, now more puzzled than awed. Could this be the collected evidence from the early days of the church, the artifacts that proved the truth claims he had tried and failed to pronounce with conviction on his mission? He files past more boxes. "Smith Family Jehovah Parchment." "Liahona." Rell stops. He turns around to find the man behind him, inches away, looking up into Rell's face with the radiance of a grinning child, sweat beaded above his upper lip. "What about the Golden Plates?" Rell asks. He looks around. "But the prophet was supposed to have . . ."

". . . given them back to the Angel," says the man. "Yes, that's the story. We couldn't possibly have scientists crowded about the ur-text of The Book of Mormon, taking their pot shots, casting doubt. In the story is where the truth lies, not in the relic, Brother Jensen." The man pauses, deliberately, as if by dangling a secret in front of his new initiate it will prolong his own ecstasy. Finally, he whispers. "The Golden Plates are here!"

There is the sound again, low-pitched but loud—four beats this time instead of five, the melancholy call. Rell moves toward the corner. He can hear wings beating violently against brick. The brilliant light dims to a pathetic lingering, fluorescent bulbs humming. *What am I doing here?* Rell thinks. *I don't belong here. Gonna get caught.* The sound continues from inside the flue, floor level, of the large chimney that rises above the building, the flue behind its cast iron door the shape and size of a television screen.

"Who is it?" demands the man, reaching for a sword from off a shelf, ancient script on its blade. Then it occurs to Rell what has happened. He brings an obscure understanding to the pinpoint of the moment, and for the first time he is about to move not because he is fleeing himself—the ultimate disappointment of an unrealized dream—but instead because he is running *to* himself.

He drops to the floor in front of the flue and places a hand flat against the metal. He can feel the bird behind it, smell the talc of broken feathers. He has heard of confused birds falling into chimneys, but always they were starlings, or maybe a robin. But a raptor?

"Get me some gloves. Are there gloves down here?

"What is it?"

"A bird."

"That is most certainly *not* allowed," intones the man, raising the sword.

"Give me your jacket," Rell demands. He thrusts out his hand. The man looks at Rell with rage, the heavy sword changing hands, the tip finally dropping to the tile floor with a clang. He sheds the jacket and hands it over to Rell.

"If word gets out about this," says the man, "I'll be fired, excommunicated!"

"Now stand back," replies Rell. "It is very frightened." Rell doesn't know exactly what he is doing. He's seen the gauntlets worn by falconers, the hoods on the heads of hawks to calm them. But this . . . this is a frightened, and probably injured owl—a Great Horned Owl he has long supposed by its call—an animal perhaps never touched by human hands. He could phone animal control, maybe even the nearby aviary, but then there is the room, this room with all its cache.

Uninvited, in his mind, Rell is a child again. "What happened to the golden plates?" he is asking his father during morning scripture reading. The staid response does not satisfy the young Rell. "Why?" he demands. "Why did the prophet have to give the plates back to the angel?"

"So that we would have to accept the truth of things on faith," his father rejoins, and the way his father moves at the table, alternating between his bowl of cracked wheat and his reading aloud from the tissue-thin paper of his scriptures strikes the boy as coy, tentative. But his father's word is never just confident, but always certain.

So Rell took regularly to his dreams. In dreams he was ushered into a buried chamber of artifacts from ancient America. There were parchments and inscribed metal plates—and implements like the *urim and thummim* designed to read them.

If there was tangible evidence that proved the Truth, why not collect it? Why not follow the impulse of the biblical Job to etch in giant stones the revealed truth? What good was the truth if you couldn't transfer it like fruit picked from a tree and give it to others? But that was then, before he woke up and all of it was too real, too raw, too disappointing, and he took to the bottle. Now he is counting his days as the program says. "One day at a time."

Rell knows only one thing at this moment. His father was right. Faith could only be maintained if there were uncertainty, and whether the relic was real or simply from the fiery imagination of a nineteenth-century mystic, did not matter. This room would remain undiscovered.

He takes the jacket and wraps his left hand in it and then slowly opens the flue. Out tumble the dreams, dead now or dazed, lying under the weight of the bird or individually crawling out on the floor in one last turn to their place of final rest. And then there is the owl, its right wing still bent up the interior of the chimney—the remiges frayed—the other wing crumpled beneath its body. The reddish facial disc shows in the dark like a moon unto itself. On its throat is the distinctive white patch. Its underbelly, light with brown barring, trembles in the refracted moonlight from above. And there are its talons and the brick scratched raw.

The man staggers back at the sight, sword once again raised, the moon-faced bird lying akimbo but somehow intact in the bottom of the flue and spilling into the room. Rell coos. "Come along, now. I'm not going to hurt you. Don't be afraid," and he slides his other hand into the jacket and slowly moves it. The bird's eyes remain placid as if this ungainly happenstance were natural.

When Rell reaches under the owl's breast, it screeches and pumps its wings, violently. Rell falls backwards, covering his face as the bird dislodges itself and expands to its former size, wings spread, beak open, talons ready. The man grips the sword harder, raises it higher.

"Kill it! It will destroy the relics!" he screams, then drops the sword to the tiled floor, inches from where the bird has landed momentarily before flapping awkwardly back up, feathers of the injured wing now at notched right angles.

"Back off!" shouts Rell to the man who is getting ready to take a second swing. "Back off, you asshole!" The sword lowers again but this time with a sick thud, and the bird half flies, half scrambles to the corner by the door, its breast smudged with old soot, eyes still mechanical and wide.

The man is bleeding. The sword has fallen to his foot, cut through the canvas and half-severed a toe which lies bloodied in the shoe's box. The man stares at his foot. Rell stares at the bird, tiny now next to the shelves of relics, its wings collapsed. He moves toward the animal, jacket in hand. Gently, he hoods the bird with the sleeve, then wraps the remainder around its body. He makes sure the wings are folded in, the jacket between the talons and his hands like a falconer's fist. Slowly he stands with it, protected in his arms.

With the bird secure, he turns to the man who is sitting on the floor, now holding his foot and rocking, the thin hair of his head ruffled forward in two pointed tufts. The sword lies at rest on the floor. The man begins to weep.

"Put pressure on it," says Rell. "You'll be okay. We'll get you to a doctor. Do it!" The man takes off his sock, bunches it and presses the dry part to his foot with a wince. He stops crying, and in his face Rell can see the man's pain dissolving before him into fear. For a moment, Rell considers leaving the bird wrapped in the jacket and just walking out of the strange building, out through the gate, out of the city and into the mountains—anywhere with a fifth of Jim Beam where he can nurse his own residual fear, his default, instead of another's. But he knows that in this place it is his own anguish he is faced with, and that this man is a kind of brother. So Rell will stay. He doesn't need to say it to the man, but he does.

"You can tell them you were here because I called you, because of the noise in the basement. The Brethren don't have to know anything about this." The man nods numbly.

Rell turns and moves up the stairs. The heat from the bird beats through the jacket against his chest. He is careful not to jostle the package, the owl's head half-surfacing, its great horns peering up out of the jacket in the yellow light.

Outside, Rell prepares to release the bird, to see how it does in the open. The pavement is wet from the silenced sprinklers, the grass beside it bejeweled so that the red bricked Telegraph & Telephone Exchange-turned-Church-book-depository is the only home he needs right now. *This is my reward*, thinks Rell. *For my sobriety. That I saw the relics of my long-lost faith.*

A familiar pride again enters his heart.

As Rell leans down to unwrap the swaddling, the great horned owl screeches again and in a single move that reasserts everything Rell suspected about the universe, rakes its talons across Rell's face.

Everything is raw; everything is present.

Rell cries out, both hands to his face. The owl struggles momentarily to free itself from the jacket, dropped to the ground, but then is still. "I was trying to free you," cries Rell. The bird looks up at him, its eyes the watery embodiment of the whole world. "I was trying to free you," he repeats, wrapping the jacket back around his fist and lowering it to the bird, which alights on it, and bringing himself to his full height, Rell lifts the bird, and, after the slightest pause in which he considers who this might determine him to be, he accomplishes the cast from his makeshift fist into the air with the authority of a seasoned hawker. The owl flies, barely clearing the spiked fence, over the median of grass under the locust trees and elms, higher above 7th East, then north, back toward Gilgal.

In the parking lot of the depository, Rell stoops, holding his hand to his face, wetness on his cheeks. If he had wings he would follow the owl to wherever it went, it wouldn't have mattered. But now, sitting on the asphalt, the hum of the crime lights re-established in this strange but honest place, he knows he is designed to be here on the ground, in his own garden, and he knows now he can start the planting.

Unexpectedly back at Gilgal, the owl waits for the sphinx to awaken. "Did he find his treasure?" asks the sphinx finally.

"No," says the owl, looking about the place. "And the garden, it can't be safe like the good sculptor hoped, can it?"

"Safe for what? Safe *from* what?" asks the sphinx. The owl is silent for a moment, then it takes its leave.

The owl flies from the garden of stone, under the dark outline of tree branches, into the street, high above houses and shops, past the deserted streets of downtown, the theaters and bars quieted and forlorn. The mountains are a different blue now that the moon has moved further west, a single silhouette still implacably drawn as with a pencil to the east. It darts to Liberty Park, to the aviary, where the native intern greets her. She smells of blood and her talons are stained red.

"You were supposed to collect the dreams of the city, and instead it looks like you've just come back from dinner," says the intern, as he returns the owl to its cage.

Caliban Revels Now Ended

The nineteenth-century copy of Shakespeare's plays, binding brittle, pages yellowed with age, sits out West now, on Ethan's desk. The old man gave it to him in the summer of 1981.

Ian's house stood atop a slight hill on Grove Street Extension in a small New Hampshire town. He had spent his life as a carpenter, and many of his old tools rusted away in dark corners of his barn, attached to the house New England-style. Inside there were at least a hundred feet of shelved books. Everything from Milton to Dreiser and from old Sears catalogs to engineering manuals. Ethan often stopped to admire the collection.

Ethan and his missionary companion "Elder" Myers had tracted into Ian one day while making their rounds in a town where Brigham Young had once converted an entire Baptist congregation to Mormonism, moving it *in toto* out West. But now the Boston Massachusetts Mission was the lowest-baptizing mission in the states, or so it was said. So when Ian let them in the door, they were grateful. Since Ian had suffered a stroke three years earlier, the two young missionaries had to help him move up or down the stairs and around the house. He couldn't speak or even hold a book.

The missionaries didn't have anything else to do, so they quickly fell into a habit of visiting Ian every morning for half an hour to read the Book of Mormon to him. They logged the visit as part of their study time. They were strange mornings, two twenty-year-olds reading to an old man who hadn't spoken a single comprehensible word to them—emitting only coughs and wheezes.

> *And in that day shall the deaf hear the words of the book, and the eyes of the blind shall see out of obscurity and out of darkness. And the meek also shall increase, and their joy shall be in the Lord, and the poor among men shall rejoice in the Holy One of Israel.*

Ethan often wondered if they were wasting their time—not to mention Ian's. Did he even understand what they were reading? They tried explaining to him that the Book of Mormon was scripture, like the Bible, but that it was an ancient history of the Americas. Ian would only nod and stare at them with the wide eyes of a person locked in intractable fear. Could he comprehend that they were reading to him about an alleged visit of Jesus to the ancestors of the Native Americans? They didn't know. But still, the two of them kept going back, and he would always be waiting.

Most of the house was closed off, except for the kitchen, Ian's upstairs bedroom, and Bill's room. Bill was Ian's housekeeper, hardly younger than Ian though much more able—a husky, slow man whose life of hard manual labor seemed to show in the deep creases of his face and in his fatigued movements. Bill cared for Ian, cleaned the house, and prepared meals in exchange for his room and board. He seemed happy to have Ian off his hands for a half hour every morning.

Soon after their visits began, the two missionaries were mentioning Ian in their companionship prayers before leaving their apartment for the day's work. They brought him foreign postage stamps that came from their missionary buddies stationed around the world. Ian accepted them for his collection which he showed the two young men, mutely as always but, despite the wild eyes, with a smiling sense of pride.

While mounting the stairs, the missionaries would hear Ian clumping around, turning off the radio, straightening the bed, slowly opening the door to let them in. The room became familiar to them that spring and summer—the battered TV in the corner, the crumpled, yellowing newspapers on the floor next to the chair Ethan always sat in, the smell of dirty blankets and stale air. When they finished, Ian would always stand and shake their hands. Ethan could never forget the feel of a hand with only three and a half fingers—a reminder of Ian's past vocation.

There was something about reading the verses aloud—the way they filled the old house with an authoritative cadence—that conjured for Ethan an assurance he hadn't felt before: that the book was a good one; that it was speaking to him. One day, the words expanded rich and full in the still bedroom, and Ethan's voice trembled under their weight. But Ian would only whimper now and again, his expression still stunned by a paralyzed face.

Outside of prayers, the missionaries rarely mentioned their early morning meetings with Ian. For Ethan it felt as if their acts there were sacred, like doing temple work or dressing a body for burial. To Ethan it seemed irreverent to talk much about it.

❧

During one of their visits, the missionaries were startled to hear approaching footsteps. Not Bill's shuffling steps—lighter ones. They stopped reading. The door opened. A middle-aged woman stood in the doorway. Ian couldn't introduce her to them, but Ethan was sure it wouldn't have mattered. He could tell from her suspicious look at their name tags, white shirts, and trademark short hair that they were not welcome.

"Uncle Ian, are these men bothering you?" she asked.

She wore a business suit; her dark hair coyly framed her face and belied her forceful manner.

Elder Myers introduced themselves to her.

"We're missionaries . . ."

"I know who you are. And I need you to leave now." They excused themselves, said goodbye to Ian, and left.

"Susan is Ian's niece," Bill told them on their way out the side door through the attached barn that now served as a garage. "She makes it up from Nashua about once a month." They listened to her voice, rising and falling above them. Ethan was certain that she viewed them as insensitive at best, conniving and manipulative at worst. In spite of the reputation that certainly preceded them, thought Ethan—to baptize as many as they could for the glory of the kingdom—they weren't there for a convert, were they? Ian, that sick, seemingly lonely man ready to pass on? But then, why were they there? To warm themselves in the dry heat of the wood stove Bill stoked downstairs? To be anywhere but in the cold, drab missionary apartment across town with the teaching pool poster on the wall that had no other name on it but Ian's? They weren't technically teaching Ian . . . just reading from a book that they were boldly proclaiming to be scripture to a world that didn't seem to care.

Despite the niece, the missionaries walked back to Ian's house the next day, not because they were fearless or unembarrassed, but because their daily visit had become a reassuring habit. Morning studies, prayers, breakfast, then Ian for thirty minutes before trudging door-to-door for the rest of the day.

As they rounded the corner of Grove Street Extension, they saw Ian waiting up for them, peering out at them through his bedroom window, his white hair reflecting the light of the morning sun.

And it supposeth me that they have come up hither
to hear the pleasing word of God, yea, the word
which healeth the wounded soul.

❧

The cold spring molted into summer, and the days became long and uncomfortably humid. Soon the gypsy moths were out, laying waste the foliage. As they walked door-to-door along the sparsely populated streets and the outlying roads that burrowed through tall trees, Ethan could actually hear the steady crunching of the millions of devastating larvae.

Once when they were out prospecting for potential new converts—"turning over rocks"—they called it, Ethan tried to convince Elder Meyers to climb a tree. "You can't tell where you are out here," Ethan argued. "You have to get up high."

"Then why don't you climb the tree?" Elder Meyer retorted. He was from Ohio—flat, compared to Ethan's mountainous home of Idaho.

"I think I might be afraid of heights," Ethan replied, lamely. "At least the ones in New Hampshire."

Elder Meyers gave Ethan his stack of tracts to hold and tucked his tie protectively inside his short-sleeved white shirt.

The gypsy moths munched in an unrelenting monotone all around them. Occasionally, one would drop from its thread to the ground where Ethan would mash it underfoot. When his companion had climbed up about thirty feet, he shouted down.

"Too many trees. Can't see anything." No new rocks visible from up there to turn over.

❧

They didn't report much to mission headquarters in Boston. And they never reported their hours with Ian. He didn't fit in any category on their spreadsheet, not even as someone to whom they provided a "Teach and Testify" (fifty per week being the quota).

Even so, they returned daily. And one day, Ethan went back to say goodbye.

"I'm being transferred tomorrow to a different area." He told Ian. "I'm going to work at the mission headquarters in Cambridge. They don't give us much time, you know; just twenty-four hours is all." He could hear Bill downstairs cleaning up the breakfast dishes. "I'd like to leave you my card, if that's all right," he continued, handing him his personalized Articles of Faith card, which seemed impersonal for the situation—tacky, even. Ian lifted it to his eyes, turned, and then clumped down the stairs.

Ian must have heard Ethan mention his love of Shakespeare, or perhaps the old man remembered how often Ethan admired the collection in the house of antique books, because Ian decided that the Complete Works would be an appropriate gift.

Ian held Ethan's hand a bit longer than usual, and then shuddered as the missionaries picked up their books to go.

Elder Meyers promised to return with his new companion. They left Ian standing at the upstairs window as usual, his hand pressed against a small rectangular pane. As they rounded the corner of Grove Street Extension, Ethan looked back for a moment, but Ian was gone.

The missionaries never finished reading the Book of Mormon to Ian, and Elder Meyers was transferred himself the month after Ethan left.

❧

Nearly twenty years later, Ethan visited the New Hampshire town, this time as a journalist to cover an anniversary production of Shakespeare's *The Tempest* in the town's famous barn theater. He found the street and parked his rental car in front of what used to be Ian's house, the bright yellow paint on the clapboards now covered over with something more subdued. Ian had to be dead by now, and things had certainly changed for Ethan. He had been through a divorce and a wrenching separation from orthodox belief. He now read more of Shakespeare than of the Book of Mormon, which he was more inclined to regard as a crude, nineteenth-century document from the brilliant mind of an American mystic-turned-prophet than as a factual account of the ancient Americas. A book that most people would eventually seem to know of via another crude vehicle, related to the book only by name. A Broadway musical.

Ethan backed up the car and drove away from Grove Street Extension for the last time. His marriage not only to his wife but to the religion of his childhood had come to an end. But there was the language of marriage and of the tenacious tradition of his choice that still told him who he was as does a dream. *"Our revels now are ended . . ."* recalled Ian from that night's performance, the words of Caliban, half man-half monster, who stood duly in his rough and damned demeanor:

> *And, like the baseless fabric of this vision,*
> *The cloud-capp'd towers, the gorgeous palaces,*
> *The solemn temples, the great globe itself,*
> *Yea, all which it inherit, shall dissolve*
> *And, like this insubstantial pageant faded,*
> *Leave not a rack behind.*

Still, as Ethan drove away that summer night, he hoped that someone had read one of the final passages of the Mormons' book to Ian before he passed on—a passage that, to Ethan seemed to transcend both orthodoxy and disbelief.

> *I am mindful of you always in my prayers, continually*
> *praying unto God the Father in the name of his*
> *Holy Child, Jesus, that he through his infinite goodness*
> *and grace, will keep you.*

Acknowledgments

Thanks to BCC Press for validating work that dates back to 1986, especially my editor Heidi Naylor and copyeditor Braxtyn Birrell. For the titular story I owe a debt of gratitude to the late Lavina Fielding Anderson and to editor Kristine Haglund for green-lighting it in *Dialogue: A Journal of Mormon Thought*. Also, gratitude to actor/retired theater professor Ron Frederickson for doing a performance of an earlier version of it at the 2004 Sunstone Symposium.

Others whom I need to thank are Lisa Torcasso Downing for help with "Dreamcatcher" and Paris Anderson who first published a version of it through his series of Handmade Books.

Previously published stories in earlier iterations include "Flying Bishop" in *ellipsis... literature & art*; "Damascus Road" in mappingliteraryutah.org; "City of Saints" in *Dialogue*; "Lana Turner Has Collapsed!" in *The Path and the Gate*; "Stairway to Heaven" in *Moth & Rust* and a nonfiction version of "Caliban Revels Now Ended" previously titled "Grove Street Extension" in *Sunstone*.

At my elbow as inspiration, critics, and unofficial editors: Stephen Carter, Larry Menlove, Katherine Bahr who, as judge, placed the collection in the Utah Original Writing Competition, Levi Peterson and, most of all, my wife, Cheryl Catherine Pace, an Episcopalian who has endured with a tortured "post-Mormon" for over thirty years and was and is always my first reader, first editor, first wrangler, and always my first love.

About the Author

David G. Pace is the author of the novel *Dream House on Golan Drive*. His creative work has appeared in multiple anthologies, including *The Path and the Gate, Blossom as the Cliffrose*, and *Moth and Rust*, among others. He makes his living at the University of Utah in Salt Lake City as a science writer.

Photo credit: Todd Anderson

Made in the USA
Middletown, DE
16 August 2024